Nough ㄱ

Nought To Sixteen

Judy Goate

Cover Design by Judy Goate

Printed in Great Britain
First Published in Great Britain in 2021

In loving memory of Mummy and Granny

Acknowledgments

Thank you to all of you that took the time to add a little something to make this a better story. My love, admiration and gratitude goes to my husband Robert – you ignited my fire, and keep the flame burning. Huge thanks also to Claudette, Luis, and Dessie – for all you did, and didn't say at the beginning. Finally thank you all for coming on my journey. I'd welcome your feedback so please take a few moments to provide a review for future readers.

Note: Some of the names of character's in the book have been changed, but the essence of their contribution remains intact.

About the Author

Judy Goate took early retirement from her career due to illness. A graduate with a BA Hons. and an MBA, she worked for over a thirty-years in broadcasting. She is most importantly a wife, and mum to three beautiful children and a grandchild. She enjoys a quiet time being creative in her home in Kent.

In her first book, Judy reminisces about her childhood, living with chronic illness, and life in Hackney, east London during the 1960's and 1970's.

Table of Contents

Fifteen

We'd been talking about this night for weeks and finally it was here, my sister's 16th birthday party. Such a big deal for her, but an even bigger deal for me as Michael was going to be there. We'd come into contact a few weeks earlier at Monday Club and I knew he was the one. My one. He was tall, sleek and really good looking. He was the kind of guy that made the girls stop talking when he passed us by. It was unconscious. "Let's have a moment's silence for the glory that's Michael," the look would say. We all did it. It was a telepathic recognition that he was the 8th wonder of the world. It was a usual Monday night club which was crowded with the kids of the area. The lights were low, and the pumping beat of the latest reggae tunes were blaring out of two massive speakers sitting in each corner of the room. Two whole hours of socialising with friends while eyeing up the opposite sex. I stood against the wall of the club quietly looking around, lost in my thoughts, while I nodded along to a magical record.

It was 1978 in London, and an explosion of local talent had revolutionised reggae in the UK. Out of the blue, 'Lovers Rock' was born, which was my kind of reggae. The catchy melody and smooth sound of Janet Kay oozed out of the speaker and I found myself unconsciously nodding along. "I've got no time to live this lie, I've got no time to play, your, silly games . . ." she sang, hitting impossible falsetto notes that could break a wine glass. I watched people laughing and joking as I hummed along to the record. I was a watcher, thank goodness as, well, I had a small problem in that I had no friends, apart from Maria, but that's another story. You see, I went to the only grammar school in Hackney which, while being an academic achievement, was also the kiss of death for my social status. In fact, I had absolutely no public profile. Why? Because it was an all-girls school filled with the elite females of the local Orthodox Jewish community, with a small gaggle of white, plus a handful of black pupils. Although we were nearing the eighties, racial integration at my school was sparse. Of that minority, I was one of two that lived locally and the only one who lived on a council housing estate. The odds of me having friends that I could relate to, were stacked against me - didn't really see that coming when I passed my Eleven Plus exam. Fortunately, I was able to claim some sort of street cred, as my elder sister went to the local comprehensive school and was a bad-arse. As a result, I mostly hung around her friends, somewhere in the back. Ok, so to say that I had 'no' friends was a bit dramatic, but they probably wouldn't have given me the time of day if it wasn't for my sister, and that can be a bit crushing on the self-esteem. But I didn't dwell on it, I just made it work.

Tonight, that huddle of girls lined the walls of the youth centre. We were waiting to be asked for a dance by one of the guys that filled the opposite wall and there I was, trying to make myself small, so as not to irritate my sister. She hated that I hung around with her friends, always around, watching her every move – or so she thought. I was tapping my feet and enjoying the latest record that the DJ had put on when, suddenly, Michael came up to me and offered me a can of drink. He had to push past my sister and her friends to get to me. TO GET TO ME! I looked behind me, just to make sure that he wasn't talking to someone else in the crowd, but there was only me. This is when I found out that black people can blush. For the first time in my life, it was all eyes on me as I stood there, dumb, mute and panicked as he looked down at me. It was dark so I couldn't see him properly, but his outline was visible. I envisaged his beautiful clear, tan-coloured skin and muscular, but lithe physique. As he stood in front of me, his afro framed his head in a perfect halo. He looked a bit like Jesus in the shadows that surrounded us, which was fitting as he was revered like a saint. "Don't forget to breathe," I said to myself as I realised that I'd been gormlessly standing there for way too long, staring up at

Michael, frozen and literally about to pass out from lack of oxygen. My arm went out and I took the drink, then took a stick of gum that he offered and then, something unbelievable happened. He asked me to dance. "I couldn't, didn't," I thought. I stared a while and then surprised myself by saying "yes." He grinned his lopsided grin and handed my drink to someone or another as he led me out into the dance floor. He pulled me close (Oh my god he smelt sooooo good), and we began to dance. All eyes were on us as he leaned forward and whispered into my ear, "close your eyes and let me show you what to do". So, I did.

As we swayed in time to the music, I was lost. Everything else in the room faded away and I was transported back to the first time that I actually met him over a year ago.

***

It was Saturday evening, and we were walking towards the house of one of my Mum's oldest friends, Elsa. We were attending her latest 'cook out', and she welcomed us with big hugs and a smile when she opened the front door of her house. She ushered us inside, told us to put our things in one of the kid's bedrooms, and ordered us to have something to eat. Her husband Larry was at the barbecue burning the living daylights out of strips of meat, and he turned his head and waved a blackened spatula in our direction. People were everywhere, mostly Elsa's family, and a few friends, which to be honest was as much people as the house could take. Elsa had eight children, as did her sister Eve, and her other sister had five boys, all of which looked exactly the same, even though they were two sets of twins and one extra. Elsa also had a set of twin sons, but the rest of her kids were girls. Larry also had a big extended family, with what felt like hundreds of nieces and nephews which ranged in ages, from newborn babies to teenagers like me. They were a friendly, loud and passionate family who all talked over each other and laughed a lot. I saw Brenda, one of Elsa's daughters that was the same age as me, and I smiled.

My Mum had unceremoniously dumped our cardigans, jackets and her massive canvas handbag in my arms and I nodded down at the pile, indicating to Brenda that I needed to know where to put them. She made her way to the bottom of the stairs and I followed her up into one of the bedrooms. Inside, I saw bunk beds and a group of boys hunched over, in a huddle on the floor playing 'jacks'. They were throwing tiny star-shaped metal objects up into the air and trying to catch them on the backs of their hands before they hit the floor. The jacks that they didn't catch were picked up with a small rubber ball and a lot of skill. I became distracted as a kid had reached ultimate genius as he had thrown up and caught ten jacks. There were shouts of "fix, no, no, no!" and "whaaaa!" from the other boys. Even I had to stop and admire the move, as it was unheard of. "Jeez, that's hard-core," I thought absently as I plonked our stuff on the top bunk. I had only ever been able to catch six in one go. I screwed up my face as a whiff of 'boy funk' hit me full in the nose. The mix of sweat, feet and something only boys seem to ooze

5

was familiar to me, as my brother had the same smell. "This must be the twin's bedroom," I thought, as I made a hasty retreat and ran downstairs with Brenda.

There was a lounge and a dining room which was full of Elsa's family and held many people of all ages organically moving together as one organism. The Elders were seated in the various chairs gossiping and over-seeing the babies and the young ones, shooing them away from the table which was filled with food. Homemade coleslaw and salad sat to one side and a massive pot of rice sat in the middle with mats underneath it as it had just come off the stove. There was hard dough West Indian bread, bula cake, shop bun, fruit cake and the first batch of meat from the barbecue. Elsa's family came from Guyana and with that, came quite specific food familiar to that country. Pig foot souse was an island favourite, which was pickled and jellied meat, served cold and flavoured with pepper. Chow Mein made with shrimp and mixed frozen vegetables was one of my favourites. But I didn't get along with escovitch fried fish with onions and peppers. Way too much pepper and bones for my liking. Today's prized offering was Larry's seared meat, with his special rub that was a well-guarded secret. He always seasoned the meat from the night before and would baste it regularly, to give it its unique smokey flavour. It looked burnt and black when it came off the barbecue, but it was actually really, really juicy and soft and I couldn't get enough of it.

The aunties served the children first and then the older kids and adults would move in to eat. Everybody loved to eat and sidled up to the table, filling their plate to over-flowing. There was an easy silence in the house while we all chewed and hummed and haaaed about nothing in particular. It was all part of the eating ritual to let the cooks know that they had 'done good'. It was washed down with sorrel and sarsaparilla, and slowly the noise of the family would start to come to life again, trying to compete with the calypso that was blaring out of the gram that was in the corner of the living room. The younger kids hovered near to the record collection with a pile of music that they wanted to play. It never happened. Nobody wanted to hear Gregory Issacs or Bob Marley. It had to be music from 'back home'.

I hung around, on the fringes, not really a part of things, as I wasn't really related to anyone. But at the same time, I remained connected as I had to call all the adults aunty and uncle as though we were clan. Now that the food had been cleared away, Uncle Malcolm and his wife Velma started to dance, and in the dining room, dominoes began. White rum and brandy started to flow, and the men sat around the table contemplating their next move. Always the men and never ladies. I noticed that I probably wouldn't ever be able to get a seat at the table and play, because that wasn't the point. The point was that it was a show, a serious concentration of manliness, all rolled into dominoes tiles. Each move was accompanied by a raised arm high in the air before it was slammed down hard on the table triumphantly. Always accompanied with a laugh or a grin as dropping that tile meant that someone was one step closer to winning the pot of money that was stashed on the side of the table. I was hooked. I loved the whole idea of a game becoming a spectator sport, with banter and laughter running side by side with competition and defeat. It was all done in good taste, but lord, was it loud. As the drink flowed, things became more raucous and less playful and I moved away towards the bedroom to get my cardigan. My mum had gone home earlier with my younger brother and sister and I could see my older sister motioning across the room that it was time to go. She had been in the living room with the teenagers who had finally gotten control of the gram and were playing the latest sound, including Michael Jackson's new album Off the Wall, which I loved.

In the bedroom, I wandered around trying to find my red cardigan under a sea of blankets and clothes on the top bunk. It was just like when we went to the launderette and all the clothes became a muddled heap. As I yanked at something that looked familiar, I turned around exasperated, as it was someone's jacket. It was then that I noticed a boy. He was slightly older than me, taller than me, and was actually looking straight at me. He greeted me and I narrowed my eyes suspiciously. "How did he know my name?' I thought, as I looked around and saw that the room was empty. I started to panic. I couldn't quite work out why he'd chosen to speak to me, and I started to shuffle from foot to foot - a small movement. He was lounging in a chair near the door and smiled a lopsided smile. As he watched me intently, I suddenly became aware that I was staring, not speaking, and that I looked like an idiot. I found myself panicking even more and wished that I'd worn something a little more appealing than my Bay City Rollers tee shirt and hand me down jeans.

"I've been wanting to talk to you for ages" he continued casually, and my head jerked up with a start.

"What the hell," I thought desperately, standing there like a lemon. I had to do something, and I had to do it quick. "Yeah? So why didn't ya then?" I thought about saying and instantly rejected it. Or should I say, "took your time didn't ya?" Once again that was rejected. I thought about what I could say that would have been less… combative? aggressive? angry? more decent? At this point I wanted to die. My first real conversation with a boy and I'd nearly come across like I was a smart-arse.

I still hadn't spoken, and the silence was beyond the point of decency. While I was thinking about how stupid I must look, I saw him sneak a glance at his watch. And then, I burst out laughing. He looked up sheepishly and gave me a quizzical look as he had no idea what I was laughing at. I quickly explained that two minutes earlier, I'd done exactly the same thing and wasn't looking forward to the reaction I would get either. My sister and I should have left Elsa's ages ago and we knew that we were gonna be in serious trouble when we got home.

He then howled with laughter, as I had read his mind to the letter. After awhile he murmured "I don't mind what happens, if it means that I can get to speak to you". WHAAAAT! Suddenly it got weird again. This was way too much, too fast, too soon. I decided to bury my hands in the clothes on the bed to create a distraction, and as if by magic, my groping hands found my cardigan. I turned away to pull it out from the mound on the bed, and to hide my face, which would have probably shown the confusion that I felt. I couldn't process what'd just happened and I needed to get away as quickly as possible. Awkwardly, I made my way to the door and after looking into his eyes for a moment, I said, "see ya," and was gone. Then in a heartbeat I quickly returned to the room and asked in an offhand way, "what's your name again?"

"Michael," he replied. And then I ran downstairs and left.

***

Michael and I hadn't spoken again - until now, a year later. And here I am, floating on a cloud of happiness in a dingy corner of the local youth club. I seriously felt like Cinderella. He picked me to dance with him, out of all the girls in the youth club. Does that make me the belle of the ball? I thought so and as I danced, I wished for the moment never to end.

And then, the spell was broken as I was unceremoniously wrenched out of Michaels arms. I opened my eyes to see my furious sister telling me that it was time to go. Of course, it wasn't, as the club had another fifteen minutes before it was due to finish. I looked at her blankly, just to make sure that I'd heard her properly, and my protest died on my lips. She was majorly pissed and, she was in charge. I could tell by her stance and the tilt of her head slightly to one side that dissent was not an option. There was a golden rule that all second born kids had to follow - the older sibling's always in charge. If she said it was time to go, then unfortunately, it was time to go. I don't think Michael realised what was going on when, all of a sudden, he found himself without a partner, standing in the corner of the room. No explanation was offered as I was marched off the dance floor towards the exit. As my ears burned and people turned to slyly stare at my abrupt departure, I found myself in a tumble of emotions that I just couldn't process. One thing that was clear however was that my sister was not happy that I'd been asked to dance. It was obvious from a mile away that it bothered her. Hence the hasty exit.

As I walked home on that warm spring evening, I was suddenly aware of how mild it was. Everything seemed to be just a little bit brighter, more vibrant than usual, and I was aware of the tingling in my stomach which still lingered from my dance with Michael. It was the most amazing moment of my life. I looked at my sister and her friends, who interestingly, didn't look brighter or vibrant, and I knew what was going to follow. As soon as we turned out of Kingsmead Road, they linked arms and, walking in pairs, shuffled along snickering. My sister started to make little digs at my first dance, and her mates joined in. "He probably thought he was dancing with someone else cos it was way dark in there," and "We all know that he did it for a bet," were some of the remarks that they made.

"What if they were right?" I thought, "why would he want to dance with me?" I was under no illusions about the way that I looked. I was ordinary, not ugly ordinary, but certainly nothing other than average. I had average skin, not dark or light brown but somewhere in the middle. My hair was ok, it never looked great as I didn't know what to do with it and, didn't care enough to find out. I was muscular with an athletic build because of my love of sports, with well-defined legs and shoulders, which wasn't particularly fashionable. I was sometimes called 'American footballer' because of my broad shoulders and as a result my body was something that I never showed off. I didn't really care about style and always wore army cadet trousers, jeans, and more comfortable baggy clothes. I never wore make-up, dresses or platform shoes which were all the rage. As I walked, trailing behind the rest of the girls, I continued to go through my good points mentally, and I just couldn't find a reason for Michael to be interested in me. Ok, I conceded that I had long legs for my minuscule five-foot two frame and that I also had a killer waist. It was small, tiny even, and made me look like I had curves when I really didn't have much to speak of. But I wasn't stupid. I knew that the few positives that I had, just wasn't enough to make me attractive. Jeez.

I was a typical teenager grappling not only with my emotions but also my identity. It was the end of the seventies and things were starting to change within me, and all around me. I was starting to see that there was a tension and energy that young people had, that seemed to be missing in our parents. Maybe it was because we had time to explore what it was to be a teenager and they just couldn't relate, as they'd never had that luxury. 'Teenager' was not a word that they had in their vocabulary. I never heard my Mum, or my Granny ever mention the word before. My Granny was born and raised in Trinidad, a child, and then, she was an adult, just like that. There was no pause, no break. As soon as she could reproduce basically, she was expected to think about working, marriage and having children, not necessarily in that order. She had fun – loads of it – and she'd have us in stitches with some of her stories. But it seemed to me that once she reached puberty, she had to fit her life around helping to support her family, along with her siblings. Giving up her dreams as they all did, and all morphing into adulthood seamlessly, and becoming wives, husbands, parents. Granny always talked as if she didn't have many choices and had a limited future. She never got tired of telling us that. "You all have it too good over here. What the hell is a teenager?"

She drilled it into us through her stories. Every action that she'd had as a child, and into womanhood was focused on survival. She'd had to work hard to get to England. And then the reality of being here? It was a nightmare that she couldn't wake up from. She used to say, "if I could have got a ship right back home, I would have turned around and gone right back – but I couldn't. Go back to what? I had to find my way. If I didn't do it, then who would do it for me? No one."

Sometimes, as she reminisced about her arrival, she'd explain, "I came here on my own, no family, just me and a suitcase full of dreams. I had to put my head down and work hard to find my place, my home. I was living in a country that really didn't want me, other than for slave labour to fill the jobs that nobody else wanted to do. To carry their shit, their bedpans.

That was my reality, and the future of all black people who settled in England during the fifties with me." Sometimes, just sometimes, the sadness and pain of her soul would creep through in her voice and she would say, "child, I had to work haaaard, so you all could have a better life. Huh . . . You don't know the half of it..."

She was right. We didn't know real hardship. We didn't know the half of it because we lived in a different time. We lived in the seventies and went to school until we were sixteen and then the choices were many. Work, further education, apprenticeships – it was all there for us to walk into. We were optimistic and didn't have to think about money and food and the electric bill. We didn't want to think about the depressing past of our parents, we expected a better future, we probably took it for granted. We had an expectation that our lives would be bright, so we focused less on survival, and more on things of the mind instead.

For me, there was nothing concrete that I could grasp that was essentially black and British, that reflected me in a positive way. No art, no clothes, no images, no books, no politics. The only exception was music. And that became my passion.

It was the late 70's and the music scene was on fire with homegrown talent making new kinds of reggae - dancehall and lovers rock. The talent was mind-blowing. Carroll Thompson, Louisa Marks, Jean Adebambo, Sandra Cross and Sylvia Tella were representing for the girls and, the In Crowd, The Investigators, Matumbi and Peter Hunnigale was doing it for the boys. They were all local and, most of them were around my age and went to school with someone who knew someone's brother or sister from school, sports or music. That meant that they weren't 'stars' or special but were average, accessible kids making the music that teenagers in England wanted to hear. There was even talk of a new movie coming out called 'Babylon', which was hopefully going to use black artists and musicians from England, including Aswad, who I loveeeed. But that could have just been wishful thinking . . .

When sports came on the telly, it didn't matter who was participating – if they were black – we would cheer them on. Boxing and athletics especially were major events in our house. If a black man or woman won, we would cheer them on, even if we didn't know their name. Just to see a black person on the track or in the ring, meant that we would cheer them, applaud them, and feel pride. I was desperate to see more people like me on the telly, in the cinema, on a billboard or winning medals. I wanted to see black people being represented in a positive and triumphant way that came from my world. Role models were few and far between, and I was struggling to find my place in the world of Hackney, as a second-generation black immigrant, in a place called England.

While I was trying to figure all of that out, I looked around me. I couldn't see myself in context, as there wasn't anyone that looked like me in any of the magazines or on the telly. Every image that I saw was white, and it constantly told me, showed me or implied that beauty could only be measured by how 'white' someone looked. How white was my hair, how long, fine or manageable? How white was my skin, how light, or near white, with the least amount of colour as possible? It was obvious really. The nearer to white you were, the prettier that made you. To move away from that and look like a black person, implied that you were . . . not pretty. I wasn't close to white nor was my hair anything other than nappy. Well, not nappy, but ordinary. I was . . . averagely ordinary. I knew that it was wrong to see myself in that way, but I wasn't a fool. Boys would measure my beauty with the same tools that all black people around me did. Was that the truth? What was the truth?

I was a defenceless mess, confused and wondrous, all at the same time. Confused about how I felt about everything, and also happy that something good had happened to me. Did Michael like me, or was there something else going on? Too many questions and emotions were coursing through my body, and I could feel that I was reaching overload. And then 'it' happened. I felt a sliver of blood running out of my left nostril. Luckily, I had a tissue and was able to stem the flow pretty quickly but not before noting just how hot it was. Once again, I was amazed that I'd never gotten used to the feeling that is no feeling, when blood decides it has to leave your body without any warning, and without your permission. The temperature is hotter than water warmed on the stove and the speed that it descends is unbelievable. But I'd been dealing with this all my life, and I was pretty good at sensing that it was on its way out. I was always prepared and walked with tissues to make sure that I could clean myself up, without any drama or fuss. On this occasion, I went through a whole packet of 'Handy Andy's'. As the rest of the group was walking in front of me, they didn't pause, or miss a beat, because of my nosebleed. It was just what I did, all the time, and no one was freaked out or noticed my discomfort. I was a little sad that no-one showed any interest, but I was glad that I was preoccupied, because it meant that I didn't have to think anymore. It also meant that I didn't have to talk to my sister throughout the journey as I was still pissed at her. "I hope your party is a big arse flop," I muttered under my breath. Jesus, she was such a bitch!

***

Obviously, I could barely sleep that night because I was traumatised. "Did Michael honestly remember who I was? Was this dance, albeit a year later, the next stage in our relationship? Hold on a minute – are we in a relationship already?" I shook my head in disgust and pulled back my blankets as I felt a little warm. As I lay in my bed, I tried not to move around too much as I didn't want to wake my younger sister who was asleep a few feet away. We shared a room and, even though she was a few years younger than me, we got along really well. Our bedroom was divided into two. My half was full of books, with pictures that I had drawn on the wall. My sky-blue polyester bedspread with ruffles covered my pristine bed and all of my books were lined up in author order, properly dusted and immaculate – mostly

Mills and Boons romantic quick reads but some gems like Sense and Sensibility, Wuthering Heights and Great Expectations were stashed at the back. Brighton Rock, Room at the Top and Of Mice and Men were needed for school so were at the front. I sometimes felt disloyal to my old favourites that sat in a corner, on their side, so I would read them again and again and be transported to a different world, for a while.

My sister's side of the room was immaculate, with a bright pink bedspread that echoed mine. Everything in our room was tidy including our wardrobe, our shoes, even our knickers drawer. Flowers were everywhere on the blue and white wallpaper and the carpet was a mass of colour, mostly oranges and brown, and was about ten inches shy of the walls around the room. We had a large sash window, and our room was situated on the top floor of a Victorian house. It wouldn't stay open on its own during the summer and couldn't keep the cold air out in the winter. Tonight, I kept it open as I lay in bed, propping it open with a piece of wood, hoping that the fresh air would help me to clear my head. I was wrong. It did however let in a cool breeze, and a hint of perfume from the garden

Although we hardly touched it, the garden produced all sorts of flowers, bushes and greenery which was left to grow wild, year after year. Sometimes, I'd sit on my bed and stare hard out of that window, looking, searching for something more than the jungle imprint that I saw. I'd come back from my trance and refocus on my room and feel grateful that I wasn't in the wilderness on the other side of the glass. I'd feel a little trapped in the box that was my bedroom, but it was better than being on my own in the untamed garden, with its mess and lack of order. The smells reminded me of that thought that I'd once had, as I finally drifted off to sleep

The following week at Monday Club, I played pool out back with some of the guys and it turned out that I was really good at it – who knew! I'd decided to hang around the boys as I didn't have much to say to my sister's friends. We all knew the score. I had to be in their clique because that was how my sister got to hang and go out with them. Without me, my Mum just wouldn't give her the freedom that she had. So, they didn't think that I was really worth talking to and, they thought that I was weird. "Why'd your sister talk like that?" I heard one of them say to Sandra one night.

"Because she thinks she's better than us," was her reply as she looked me up and down, sniffed, and gave me a side-eye as she turned her head away as though I was an offensive smell that had caught her attention. She could be so sassy sometimes – she had it down pat. I'd catch the look and try to stare her down but couldn't. I couldn't maintain a game face and couldn't be bothered to stand up to her. Besides, I never really understood what they meant as I didn't believe that I talked differently. I mean, so what that I went to a grammar school and who cares that elocution and handwriting lessons came as standard. I was still the same person on the inside, the same as them.

I decided that girls were hard work that I could do without. They talked about hair and clothes and all the things that I just wasn't interested in. So, when I was around them, I kept my mouth shut and my head down, as girls could also be really mean I'd come to realise – your best friend one day and cut you down to the quick the next.

Hanging with the boys was uncomplicated and there was no confusion. I smoked, I could take a punch and give one back – hard, and I just slid into their groove without causing ruffles or waves. I was having fun and starting to come out of my shell, although I kept my eyes firmly on the door, so that I wouldn't miss when Michael turned up. That evening, he didn't put in an appearance. I was gutted, heartbroken as I smiled and pretended to be having a good time right up until closing time.

As I walked home, I decided that I'd overdone it. "It was just a dance for goodness sake!" I told myself over and over as tears trickled down my face. Thankfully, nobody noticed as I wrestled with the fact that I may have read too much into my connection with Michael. After wiping my eyes, I hid my disappointment by aggressively play fighting with one of the boys who was trailing behind and lived quite near to us. I even tried out some of the kung fu moves that I'd seen at the cinema, during a late-night screening of 'Snake in the Monkeys Shadow'. As I pretended to drop kick one of my attackers, I contented myself with the knowledge that I'd definitely had a moment with one of the hottest boys around, even if I wasn't quite sure of his motives. I'd managed to pull myself together by the time we got home, and I went straight to bed, determined to get a grip and forget about him. My stern talk with myself worked, and I didn't see or hear anything about Michael for awhile. And then one day, I heard on the grapevine that he was definitely coming to my sister's party.

***

Fast forward to party night and I paused to work out which of my two shirts looked best with my jeans. In truth, it didn't really matter as it was the same two tops and jeans that I'd been choosing all year. I hadn't really given clothes that much thought as it seemed like that would have been a pretty useless exercise. We didn't have a lot of money lying around in my family, and even though I had a Saturday job at the local supermarket, new clothes were a luxury which I couldn't afford. So, what was the point in wanting, when I was well versed in making do. That way of thinking had worked forever, and I just went with the flow, not wanting much, and expecting even less. On this occasion however, for the first time ever, it mattered to me. I'm not gonna lie, my social status had elevated since the event at Monday Club, to the point that a few people even knew my name. Previously, I hadn't really had a name. I was simply known as Sandra's sister. Now people called me over at Monday Club and started conversations with me. With ME! "So, green one or pink one? Hmmm . . ." I thought as I held up both the shirts in front of the mirror. I settled for a tee shirt instead as it was a hot day, and promised to be a sultry summer's evening. I'd never been so excited about a party before; the anticipation was almost stifling.

At last, all the chores were done, the food cooked, the drinks cooled in a metal bathtub, the furniture moved, and the speaker boxes were in place in the living room. The DJ was all set to go and was testing out his sound with some raw roots reggae that had an unrelenting baseline which pulsed and tested the speakers to the limit. He then played Minnie Riperton singing 'Loving You' to make sure that the top section sounded soulful and crystal clear. My Mum looked up from what she was doing and yelled, "ah wha de hell! Turn that shit down!" The DJ quickly adjusted the sound level and put on a John Holt classic 'Help Me Make It Through The Night' to get her in the mood. Even she had to laugh as the lyric hit home. My excitement was building as slowly, people started to arrive. My sister and I were talking earlier about how many people she'd invited and how many she hoped would turn up. My heart was in my mouth and my fingers and toes were crossed as I hoped she'd have a full house. Because our house was hard to get to, I did have a thought that people wouldn't come. We were off the beaten track on the south side of Hackney, which had lots of green and Victoria Park around the corner. The only way to get to the house was to walk, which people obviously thought was worth it as they started to turn up at around eight thirty.

Finally, the party was in full swing – and I'd been relegated to cloakroom assistant. It went like this. 'Knock knock' on the front door and my sister opened up screaming "hiyaaaa," to whoever was there. "Can I take your jacket, cardigan etc," which would then be chucked over to me, and off she'd go, smiling, offering drinks and being the perfect host. That wasn't how I'd seen the evening panning out, but my notoriety had diminished around some of the girls, because there was an ugly rumour going around that wouldn't go away. Apparently, Michael had mistaken me for someone else at Monday Club and had asked me to dance by mistake. At first, I'd ignored it, but he hadn't been around for a little while and I didn't know what to believe. Eventually, I'd started to doubt myself, thinking things like "it was dark in the club so he could have made a mistake . . ." or "he didn't actually say my name when he spoke to me so . . . etc. etc. etc." And this is why I hung with the boys, trying to avoid the useless gossip that only girls seemed to be preoccupied with. To me, girls were a magical poison – the kind that makes you doubt yourself, and question others.

In between taking cardigans, I ended up hanging with the guys, mucking about, being stupid while being treated like I was just one of the boys. Because it was still early, there wasn't much dancing going on yet and people were hanging around in the hallway, chatting and having a laugh. The atmosphere was good, and people seem to be behaving, chucking their cans and empty plates of food into the bags and keeping the house tidy. We needed to keep Mum sweet, because we wanted the party to go on way into the night.

I continued to keep myself busy as people began to arrive in earnest: in twos and threes like girls tend to do, and en masse

23

in packs of six, which was the boys' way of doing things. I was serving drinks, chipping ice, and picking up the odd empty cup before Mum could moan about us trashing her house. She was already getting quite stressy, constantly asking the DJ to turn the music down – which of course he did, and then it would slowly, magically, drift back up. I didn't go into the room where all the dancing was taking place. It was really dark and mysterious, and I became instantly shy of drifting into what looked like Aladdins cave. A mood had been created and I could just about make out who was who, as they jiggled and jumped to the DJ's selection. Currently Evelyn King was blaring out, singing 'Shame' – one of those records that made you move your body, even if you couldn't dance a step. It was infectious. "Back in your arms is where I wanna be . . ." I sang along, toe tapping and could feel that people were really starting to loosen up. My Mum, on the other hand, was winding up like a spring and then, without warning, she came into the living room and turned on the main light. This was greeted with moans and groans and instantly killed the party vibe. We managed to shoo her out of the room and a plan was hatched. The girls tending the bar kept spiking my Mums drink with brandy, just a bit, to hopefully keep her merry and onside. It worked, and as her friends arrived and she busied herself with entertaining them, the party progressed nicely. Good music, lots to drink (non-alcoholic for us) and a wonderfully barmy night. Things were on a roll and loads of girls were coming out of the room "for air" with hair that looked like it hadn't seen a comb in weeks. That's the thing with black hair.

Add a little heat, throw in a little sweat, and your eight-inch afro becomes a two-inch curly mess in a jiffy.

I was now stationed at the bar and I looked up to see who I was serving. It was Michael. I'd given up on him turning up – but he had. His afro looked so fine and, he sported a medallion which came down to his breastbone on a chunky gold chain. His silk shirt was a mass of colours, with four buttons undone from the top. A Fendi belt topped off his sky-blue Farrah slacks and he wore a pair of patent Bali shoes that were so shiny that I could see my face in them. I paused, we stared, and without a word we went up to the living room to dance.

My Mum was suitably sozzled so didn't care whether the light was on, off or in between, and she'd stopped moaning about how loud the music was. In fact, she even came in for a quick dance herself before deciding it might be a good idea for her to lie down, instructing her friends to keep an eye out for anything 'funny'. I'd been in the kitchen for a while, so wasn't prepared for what I met.

The scene in the living room could only be described as steamy. Couples all around the room were in clinches so tight that barely a whisper of air could pass between them. Others were nursing their drinks, shouting at each other over the noise of the music, trying to be heard, while others were just swaying along with the beat while they took in the vibe. We joined the jiggling bodies just as Dennis Brown came to life through the speakers, and I could feel the electricity in the room. It was an up tempo beat which demanded that every-one sang along. We sung and we swayed and some of the guys started skanking. We formed a circle so that the intricate moves could be seen by all and cheered them on to skank their hearts out. It was like watching a fight scene in a kung fu movie that was set to music. "Money in my pocket and I just can't get no love . . ." we sang, as one dancer pulled out a move that hadn't been seen before "boo, boo, boo," cheered the gathering, and he obviously won the day – or night, I should say. The record finished, and a crowd favourite came on – a slow jam that everybody loved. "Baby I'm yours forever endlessly, I am yours forever come what may . . ." oozed The Investigators, as Michael came in close and we started to dance. Things just slowed down – I mean time warp slowed down, and became sensual in a way that I never knew that dancing could be. Our bodies responded to the beat of the music as one and I forgot about the room, the people, and the noise around us. I had never danced with another boy in my life, but I just followed his lead and then the rest just happened, in a haze. I breathed in his smell and melted. He was much taller than me, so my head lay against his chest and skimmed across his silk shirt, while he held me firmly with his arm against his body. It was us and the music, moving in a hypnotic, kinda spiritual way. We stayed together for another record and continued to dance as if we were the only people in the room.

Unbeknown to me at the time, people had started to watch us, our interpretation of dancing. My sister said that it looked 'bad'. I wasn't sure if she meant 'bad' as in badass or nasssssty when she said it, but I didn't push her to clarify. It felt poetic to me, electric, and that must have been picked up by the crowd in some way as they stopped what they were doing and stared. We broke away after the record finished and I looked around as I came back to earth with a bump to see a gaggle of girls watching us, daggers shooting from their eyes, mouths open. The light was dim, but I knew friction when I saw it. Was there also jealousy coming my way? I didn't have a chance to work out my thoughts as I was grabbed by another guy and found myself dancing with him. "Why haven't I ever noticed you before?" he whispered, as he moved around in the weirdest way, and clunked against my hip bone in a bid to try and make me believe that he knew what he was doing. I smiled faintly and gritted my teeth, to stop myself from pulling away from his grip. I looked around wildly and saw Michael lounging against a wall, smiling in my direction, hopefully waiting for me to be free. "Why me?" I thought. Bump, knock, grind, scrape continued the dance. It was beyond awkward. I looked across again at Michael as he smiled encouragingly at me and I pulled myself up to my full height of just over five foot as the record concluded. "Why not?" I then said to myself.

Michael slid in before anyone else could pull me to dance (for some strange reason there was a queue of guys waiting to do the honours), and once again we melted together. I lifted my face as I couldn't hear what he was saying properly and found myself looking into his eyes, so warm, so brown, coming closer and closer to me. "Oh my god, he's going to kiss me," I thought. I wet my lips nervously, instinctively parting them with anticipation, slowly closed my eyes and, then it happened.

The hot trickle of blood escaped from my left nostril and my eyes shot open to see his pursed lips still on a downward trajectory to mine. "No!" I shouted just a little too loudly. He pulled back and looked confused, then hurt. I must have said it louder than I realised, as a few couples had turned to us. "Oh shit, please not now," I moaned and wrenched myself from his arms and pushed my way out of the room. I left without stopping to see whether he was still standing empty handed in the middle of the room, looking like a complete idiot.

I made my way to the bathroom and lent over the bath, running water to wash away my blood, and my tears. It literally gushed out of my nose, both nostrils by this time, cascading down like molten lava. It was on fire. Never had it been so hot. I doused my face in cold water and let the blood run out. The doctors advised that I should hold my head up, tipping backwards, squeezing tightly on to my nostrils so that any excess blood could run down my throat. Obviously, they'd never had a nosebleed themselves as they wouldn't have recommended something so torturous. Hot blood sliding down your throat is like being asked to drink the blood of a dead animal, newly killed and throbbing warm. What did they think I was – a vampire? I'd tried it for awhile, gagging and choking while the blood slid down my throat. Definitely up there as one of the most unnatural and disgusting things that I'd been asked to do.

As usual, I was left to my own devices, and I put my head forward and let it flow. It felt good getting it out of my system. It was like I was overheating in my brain, like my mind was too full, as if my capacity was bigger than my body, and this was the valve which stopped me from exploding. I felt the pressure all over my body, the intenseness as the blood pumped through my veins, looking for a way out. It literally made my head hurt as it oozed, instead of bursting out like a broken dam. And I cried and bled and thought about my missed moment. Once again, it had got in my way, stolen my life, and the party went on regardless.

Half an hour later, I was still draped over the bath. The blood still poured and showed no real sign of letting up, but the pressure and headache was receding. It was always the same. This feeling of being fit to burst at any moment, without notice, without reason, or so it felt. There came a point during the nosebleed when I felt that it would be ok to stem the flow. So, I clamped my fingers across the bridge of my nose in the hope that a clot would start to form. Sometimes, I would apply pressure too soon and the clot that formed would only last for a few seconds or minutes before being washed away by the force of the bleeding. I know better now. It takes as long as it takes for that point to come where squeezing my nose can stem the flow. And I hadn't reached that point yet. Right then, I hated my nose, I hated the pool of blood that had formed at the bottom of the bath, and mostly, I hated my life. Fifteen years old and I'd never danced with a boy until tonight. I'd nearly got my first kiss too.

What was the point of living now that it had all gone horribly wrong?

I took my fingers off my nose and let the blood fow. Time passed. I heard party noises going on in the background which made me feel even more miserable. I sighed, and I let it flow. My mind started to drift. I started to think about some of the times that this had happened before, in this weird, stopping me in my tracks way.

So, this is the part when I go back to the beginning, back through my memories. I mean, what else was there to do . . .

Eighteen Months

As the party noises recede into the background, I close my eyes and drift back in time, knowing as I leaned into the bath, that my nosebleed would take care of itself. I went back to my first memory, the first time. I didn't fight the dream-like state that I found myself in, as I entered a world that was so fresh in my mind that it could have happened the day before. I decided to let my younger version of myself speak.

I was tiny. I was alone in a cot which seemed unfamiliar to me. Well, I say cot, but it was more like a cage really. It was all metal, white and cold to the touch. It also had a long angular shape with all sides towering over me, which guaranteed that there could be no escape. I had a blanket by my feet, and that was it. Me, a little blue blanket, a cot for a cage and a huge empty room. It didn't smell right – neither the blanket nor the room. I was used to welcoming smells, foody smells. But not this. I sat up and looked around, tilting my head upwards. There was something comforting about being protected by the walls that the cot provided. Being tucked away inside a sanctuary where no one could get to me.

I remember feeling something, but it's so hard to find the words when you cannot even speak, cannot form words – yet. All I had was my senses and this bubbling mass in my tummy, and no words – yet. The light was off but there was still a glow streaming into the room from the hallway, through the door. In the brown haze where everything looked the same shade of darkness, I lay very still and listened – to nothing. No sounds, no noise, nothing that I could grasp as familiar. I was looking towards the windows and saw that it was night-time, and I turned my head and stared through the window in the door. Suddenly I could see people walking. Nobody I knew, hurrying past, urgently, with purpose.

It was at that moment that I noticed that my nostrils had been plugged and that I had to breathe through my mouth with big noisy breaths. I was used to breathing through my nose - in out, in out, simple, easy breathing that I didn't have to think about. I just did it. Now it was different, an effort, a problem that had to be solved by my overloaded system. I eventually got the hang of it, but it was scary at first, not knowing how to do something like breathing. Not knowing that it would happen whether I chose to focus on it or not. The feelings in my tummy grew into a clenching knot that was twisting and turning. It felt like colic or trapped wind – I knew them both well – but, somehow different. I could feel a kind of panic rising that was like the froth in my bottle when it was shaken too much. And then, the feeling stopped.

I became aware of more changes, but I still couldn't put a name to what I felt yet. I think I may have been in shock. Who knows? I couldn't quite understand why I wasn't freaking out. Not crying or acting like the baby that I was. An infant in a crazy new world. At least, I think I would have remembered if I was petrified, because I was awake in this unfamiliar life. Wouldn't I?

But, I definitely remember that my skin was so sore, on fire, and a different colour. No longer dark and chocolate coloured, thanks to some kind of lotion. The chalky surface was itching so much, and I had no idea why. It was too dark to investigate and even if I did see what was going on, what could I do? As I looked down at my left hand which, I noticed, had a bandage wrapped around it tightly, I felt a jolt in my tummy as the mass that had been gathering momentum erupted. My mouth opened . . . But silence. Nothing came out. There was no sound that could suggest fear so crippling that it left me literally speechless, unable to breathe. There were no sounds for the turmoil that churned inside me. No way for me to describe the terror that I felt, because I had no words – yet . . . Just thoughts, feelings, but no words. It was too much, all of it.

My home and family made me, taught me, showed me who I should be, how to feel. And without warning, I'd woken to find myself somewhere else, without that. Without them. Suddenly, everything'd gone away, so who was I? Where was I? To wake up and confront so much change. So much pain. I had no words to describe it – not yet. I sunk inwards in that moment, as I could not get my feeling out. It was beyond noise, beyond tears. It was stuck – inside. Buried. I'd been left on my own, abandoned and alone, in the brown and beige night, in my cot with its unscalable walls. I stood up in my wobbly way and looked around for something, anything familiar and there was nothing. And then, everything unravelled.

As I revisit this time, things are a little cloudy, fragmented. I try to find a vocabulary for that moment, for that baby that I was – and I can't. The best that I could say is that I felt deserted, alone. I could say what my Mum would often say about me, "she was a very quiet baby, a good child, that never really cried unless she was hungry." I could say that. I could also say that I'd learnt to be quiet and never really cry throughout my childhood. And now I understand why. This place where I am now, where I'm crying so hard, inside and out, and for so long – and no one cares. This is my new home and family. No one is there for me as I face my eighteen-month-old fear of being deserted – alone. No friend or family present as I sat there in my illness, in my mess, all wet and wailing, and no one came. No one.

But, I did not have those words then. I had no words at all. Just raw unfettered feeling, taking over steadily. I couldn't even suck my thumb for comfort as I normally did, as I needed my mouth to breathe. I just sat there, looking at the door waiting for someone to come into the room, to see me. Swish, swish past they went, fast footsteps, never looking through the glass partition in the door. Heads straight while they walked quickly past my room, none of them slowing, stopping, none of them my Mummy. Where was she? Where were they all – my daddy, sister, everybody?

With all the patience and focus of a puppy in a cage, I sat, watching that door, willing my family to come in and help me as I drowned.

Eventually, someone came in. She came straight at me in a gown that seemed to be wrapped around her several times, ballooning her up in size, while wearing a mask on her face that left only her eyes on display. I looked on curiously as she leaned into the cot and, having changed my nappy, plucked me out with gloved hands. She took a seat in a rocking chair that was in the corner of the room, unnoticed by me until then. As we sat in the shadows, she gently held me on her lap, wiped my face, and fed me a bottle. I felt her warmth, her softness, her kindness and it helped. I leaned into her folds, her humanness as it reminded me of my Mum, my home, my life elsewhere. Where was the noise, the smells, the talking, cooking on the landing in the hallway of my home, the paraffin heater that stood in the corner of our room. The heater that boiled the kettle, the kettle that burnt my arm. I wanted to go home. Would I ever find my way back there? Would I find my way out of my cell I wondered, as I realised that the scent of the stranger who fed me was wrong. She didn't feel right and I knew she wasn't family, wasn't familiar

– but it didn't matter. It helped, being in her arms. She helped. She rocked as I drank noisily while gulping for air, and eventually, fell asleep.

I had no other recollection of that place or that time again. I wondered if it was a dream or if I'd imagined the whole thing. But something told me no. It was real alright, the details were too strong, too sharp in my mind and that smell was ingrained in me and never really went away. That smell of clean and tidy, beyond what was normally required

.

***

When I asked my mum about that memory many years later, she looked at me in amazement. Then she frowned like she was having difficulty pinpointing where something ended and something else started. She did that a lot, frowning I mean, as if she had to get things straight in her mind before she could talk. She sat back in the chair and I knew that she had a story to tell. I settled in, getting comfy, wiggling into the sofa properly. "Yuh was about eighteen months old," she started, "yuh had a fever tha wouldn't go down. Bac in the sixties, when yuh hav a sick child, all chilren wud get the same germs bikaaz we all slept in dem small rooms, sharing di same beds and everything. So, everyone hav measles, mumps and chicken-pocks all at di same time." She shuddered. "Lord have mercy, was nineteen with two chilren and not a lot a sense, living on di top floor of Mr Francis house. No bathroom, kitchen eena di landing, toilet outside. What a time, what a time . . . Was not the swinging sixties for mi," she muttered.

As usual, Mum would lose the thread of the story by getting hung up on a detail that really didn't matter. On this occasion, she couldn't decide whether it was mumps or measles that we had. She settled on measles as she remembered me in bed with my siblings when it came to having the mumps. That meant that it was definitely the measles. With this sorted out, she went back to the story.

"Yuh had measles like your sister," she said emphasising the word 'measles'. "But yuh seemed to tek it a bit harder than her. I kept yuh in a cold basin for a long time, but nutten seemed to work to get yuh fever down. Then the nosebleed started." At this, she put her hands up in the air, perhaps to emphasise the helplessness that she felt. "Gyal, it gushed out of yuh suh hard dat mi did think that yuh was going to die. An ambulance cum tek wi to di hospital and dem put yuh in isolation. Yuh had measles. Again, she emphasised 'measles', but this time it was less loaded, and I could tell by the way that her voice changed that she really remembered the moment.

"They took wi to Saint Ann's hospital, not too far. It was a convent in dem days, run by nuns as well as doctors," she paused for awhile, saying nothing. "It was a nice little place with pretty gardens . . . huh, spent so much time in dem gardens," she continued absently. "Yuh sat in that bed like a good girl, all alone without crying or howling like some of dem other children, because I couldn't stay in the room with you for long. I held yuh little fingers through the gaps in the cot when they would let me. Really did think dat dat was dat." She had that look on her face that people have when they get lost in a memory – soft gazed and looking way off into the distance. While telling the story, she had unconsciously grabbed my fingers and was rolling them through her own, softly beating out a rhythm that only she knew.

She would grab our hands often as kids and beyond, when watching tv or sitting close on our settee. She had so much love in that simple action, because it was unconscious, she didn't even know that she was doing it, showing us how she felt about each and every one of us. Sometimes she'd go one step too far and start to strip our nails as she clutched us during an exciting scene on the telly. We'd giggle and yank our hands away, as we knew we'd end up with no nails left if we didn't.

Then she snapped out of storytelling mode and . . . the moment was gone. At some point she'd disentangled my fingers. When she picked up the story again, she talked in a matter-of-fact kind of way. "Yuh had lost a lotta blood, so yuh had a transfusion as soon as them git to the hospital. Them gi yuh baths for yuh fever, and stuff yuh nose to stop di bleeding."

And that was it. Story telling was over. I could tell that she wasn't in the mood to talk any more, but I tried anyway. I joked, "the treatment must have worked as I'm still here!" She didn't smile back but kept looking at me, like it was beyond weird that

I could remember details of when I was a baby, when my brothers and sisters couldn't. It got me thinking that maybe it was a little strange that I could recollect my early years. My Mum said it must have been a fluke. It wasn't.

Three

As I haze back into another time, another echo of my past, I remember that I woke up startled by I don't know what, with a muzzy head that was sore. This was a different time, when I was old enough to take in what was happening to me. A time when my thoughts were less broken up and hard to access. I remember feeling really warm and tranquil, wrapped in a blanket of cosy mist. I heard the scream from a distance, like it was almost part of a dream, so I ignored it and carried on feeling good. The scream came again, this time louder, and was followed by a bright light and lots of senseless shouting. I couldn't make out what they were saying, but it seemed like it wasn't going to stop anytime soon. I thought this would be a good time to open my eyes, and once I grew accustomed to the light, I saw it. I saw me. I was lying in bed, in a pool of blood, awash with the stuff. I remember my sister screaming yet again in the background and my mother staring in the foreground, and me sitting in the middle of it all, all of us trying to take in the sight that befell us. This is what I saw.

My bed usually had some kind of flowery print sheet which lay on top of a rubber mat, just in case I wet the bed, which of course I never did. My blanket was blue or was it green? It wasn't clear, but I remember that it was quite lightweight because it was a warm summer's evening. I had one pillow covered in the same kind of flowery design as the sheet, except that it had a slightly reddish tinge. This may have been because it'd changed colour in the wash by accident, but I'm not sure. I mean, I was three years old so didn't get involved in things like washing pillowcases. Anyway, I was in a bed that was just like any other bed which I shared with my sister Sandra. She was on the inside nearest the wall and I was on the outside, nearest the door. This was to make sure that if a monster came into our room and decided to eat us, he would get to me first. He'd hopefully be filled up enough not to want to eat my sister. I remember that tale as she told it to me while she laughed and kicked me nearer to the edge of the bed.

Sandra had stopped screaming and replaced it with a whimpering sound, and I noticed that she was curled up in a corner of the bed, as far away from me as possible. "No changes there then," I thought. I looked around as everything seemed super bright, much brighter than usual, and then I looked down.

I could see why she screamed. I was covered in blood. It was on my face, my chest, my hands and my lap. I never knew there could be so many shades of red, so many shades of blood. It was on the flowery sheet that had no flowers. It was on the slightly red pillow which look like a blob as I couldn't see where the pillow started and where the pillowcase ended. There was no blue in the blanket anymore, and I could hear a steady drip, drip, drip, as blood trickled onto the lino, at the edge of the bed.

I panicked, started crying immediately, and put my arms out to my mother so that she could hold me and make it alright. Unfortunately, she backed away and slipped on the pool of blood on the floor. She fell, hard, with a kind of grunt, which made both me and my sister cry even louder. And then all hell broke loose.

I remember that during the sixties, it was not uncommon for families to live in a shared house. In our case, I think we had a couple of rooms, one of which must have doubled up as a sitting room/bedroom. Or did we all just live in the one room? I can't quite imagine things being that bad but . . . For sure I can say that we shared the kitchen which was on the landing, with the other families, and the toilet was outside. I don't think that we had a bathroom, but I'm not sure. Electricity and gas came through a meter, and the only thing that was free was water. Everyone had paraffin heaters which transformed into cookers, making sure that the kettle was always hot and ready to go. Families living on top of one another, too close, which could have been a recipe for disaster, but we made it work. After all, we were all in the same predicament – immigrant families trying to get ahead. There was a camaraderie that the kids picked up from the adults. We got along - because we had to. We also looked out for each other, and the screaming and commotion that me, my Mum and Sandra were making, had attracted the entire household.

Men came in with planks of wood followed swiftly by their wives waving useless kitchen utensils. They burst into the room and stopped short, and they stared. Then one of the men broke the trance that everyone seemed to be in, grabbed a towel that lay on the chair, and pulled me out of the bed. My Mum was a mess of tears and uselessness and had to be comforted by the other women in the room. My sister hadn't said a word, as she was coaxed out of the corner of the bed and her soiled nightclothes were removed. She'd stopped crying by now and was staring, transfixed. She stared at the mess and confusion that was playing out in front of her, as she was gently washed, the water in the basin swirling around like a moving pool of blood. My nose was still gushing blood, so someone gave the man that was holding me more cloths to try to stem the flow. He took me outside onto the landing because the room was now crowded and there was no place else to go. I remember feeling like I was in a trance by this time, lightheaded and dreamy, maybe because I had lost so much of myself, my blood? Maybe. In my haze, I noticed that I wasn't comfortable with the amount of attention that was on me. I didn't like it – the noise, the commotion, the wailing. I just wanted my Mum to hold me, to make it all better. But she couldn't, as she was too shocked herself. I still knew what I wanted though. I wanted her to be the one who was taking charge, who was barking orders, who was protecting and looking after me, in my time of need. She wasn't. Didn't. Couldn't. That caused a pain so deep that it cut into everything, right through to my three-year-old core.

Someone must've called the police and someone else must've hailed them down to take me to the hospital. I felt the fresh air hit my face as I came outside into the warm, summer's evening. Being carried in the strong arms of a stranger, with all the tenderness that I'm sure that he would give to his own child. Things were slowing down, the haze becoming a fog as my head lolled to one side. Out of the corner of my eye I could see a woman running naked down the street being chased by a really upset man. "Strange," I thought. But then, everything about that evening was strange. So, I stored it in my three-year-old mind, and duly passed out.

***

Many years later, I tried to get my Mum to talk about this time. Her memory of the event was pretty much the same as mine, apart from the point where she slipped on my blood, bawled incessantly and was absolutely useless in a crisis. Her version put her at the centre of things, made her the one that called the police and handled the catastrophe in a calm and dignified manner. Whatever. Whatever makes her happy is okay by me. Again, she could not believe that I could remember that time, but she was used to me coming out with things that made no sense to her. "Strange" she called it. "Weird" she called me.

As we talked a little more, I mentioned that I could recall a lady running down the street as I got into the police car. "Really?" she said, "Lord have mercy gyal – yuh did see dat? Dat was Cherry." She gave a little laugh, and I could tell that she was recounting the time in her mind. She carried on with the memory silently and ignored the fact that we were in the middle of a conversation, and that she was supposed to speak.

"So . . ." I prompted her back into the conversation ". . .who was the man running down the road behind her?" I asked,

"What man? Oh . . ." she paused. She thought about it for a little while, like she was deciding whether to tell me or not. When she saw that I wasn't going to leave her alone she sniffed and said, "ohh, you mean John? Dat was Cherry's husband."

"Bloody hell!" I thought. I'm really on a roll. My Mum would normally decide that she didn't like that I remembered things from so long ago, 'big people tings' she would call it, and she'd normally change the subject. But not today. She chuckled to herself and I took that as a sign that I had a green light. "So, um, why was she naked?" I continued in what I called my 'sensitive' voice. Obviously, it wasn't sensitive enough because she clammed up. Tight. Luckily an old friend of the family was present at the time and she picked up the story where my Mum left off – happily.

"Well," said Glenda. "Yuh si, it did seem dat Cherry was eena one of da rooms wid her fancy man, and John di cum home early from work – and Cherry was not eena dem room." She paused, as if to collect the details in her mind and order them. "It was late, sooo it was odd dat dat gyal wasn't eena her own room but . . ." She shrugged as if to say she didn't really know what John was thinking. "Anyway, John went to Roys room, fi git change fi di gas meter, and found Cherry eena Roy's bed, naked. Oh gooosh, what a bacchanal!" My mum was flashing Glenda urgent looks, her eyes tiny slits, gleaming, willing her friend to shut up. Glenda was in full flight however and wouldn't be silenced by anyone. I smiled encouragingly, nodding Glenda on to keep talking. "You can jus imagine di noise and confusion. Da whole house di hear fi har screaming and dem man dem shouting and carrying on." Glenda obviously thought it was hilarious because, as she put it, "Cherry had it coming, cos everybody di know dat she was messing wid Roy. Someone muss ha call the police," she said, "bikaaz it did look like murder was on John's mind." She then looked straight at me without a trace of laughter in her gaze and said, "lucky for yuh the police did deh – dem get yuh to hospital real quick." She paused and then she muttered, "da police car was fi Cherry, but your need wa more than hers." She continued to look at me before saying one more time, "lucky."

Four

M y memories moved through our phase of living in rooms in tumble down, creaking houses in north London, to living in a part of the city that was being developed. I remember that when we moved to Hackney, which was in east London, it was a different way of living – with privacy and dignity. Many of my Mum's friends were being offered similar types of property to live in, flats in large estates, and suddenly, we felt like we belonged. I could feel the tension seeping out of my parents, especially my Mum. We lived in a three bedroom flat with our own toilet, kitchen and our first bathroom. We had a bath every night for months which was the best time ever! She kept house, because she had a flat to look after, and she sent us to our bed when we were naughty or too noisy, as we now had a bedroom.

I remember that it took a bit of getting used to, having a space to call my own. I also had to get used to seeing white faces everywhere. I'd previously only come across white people in hospitals or when a landlord came to get his rent. Now they were living among us, and it felt strange to me. After a while I decided that there wasn't any real difference and that I quite liked it, other than the smells. It was easy to make friends in the estate as we all hung in the courtyard and it was impossible not to play in the huge space that was our playground. We'd play hide and seek and tag, and I'd sometimes grab my white friends if I was 'it'. They smelt differently, milky and buttery at the same time, so I would always let them go quickly, to release myself from that smell, that smell that made me feel ill. I knew the smell instantly, as I couldn't eat dairy produce without throwing up. My Mum used to force me thinking that I was just being fussy, until she realised that I wasn't making a choice, but having a bad reaction to everything dairy that came from a cow.

I also remember that as I passed the front doors of my white neighbours, that their food didn't smell good at all. Mum said it was on account that they boiled the shit out of everything. I continued to look at her for an explanation because I didn't understand what she meant. "Them eat a lot of potato an cabbage," she said offhandedly. Then continued as an afterthought as she could see that I still didn't get it, "nutten good never cum wid eating dat kinda food, bikaaz one will block yuh insides, and the other will make yuh fart like hell." She gave a little laugh at her joke and left me wondering how life would be if all I ate was potatoes and cabbage. I later learnt that they ate other things, but I never lost that image in my mind and, never really liked either potatoes or cabbage after that.

I was four, and old enough to start at the local school. I couldn't wait. I was gagging for that day because I'd had to watch my sister start a year before me, and boy was she a shit about it. The beginnings of a massive divide started to play itself out, as three of our playmates, including Sandra, started school. Things changed. I continued to play out in the courtyard all day and after school, Sandra, Pam, and Robert would join us in the courtyard and all they talked about was school. At first, it was exciting and fun to hear about the stuff that they'd learnt. But after awhile things became difficult. If we started playing chase, or hide and seek, we would eventually end up playing schools. If we played shops, we would eventually end up playing schools. If we had races, we would start to play schools afterwards. They would be the teachers. Always. They would boss us about, get their own way and were generally, just a pain in the arse. Later on, I came to realise that they hadn't turned into bossy monsters because of school as I initially thought. Nope – they were just bossy monsters.

How could they be so powerful? Have such control over my playtime life? As I was a kid, I couldn't answer that question, but I intuitively knew that things had changed, and it had everything to do with school. In the meantime, it was really just a case of 'put up' and 'shut up'. We were three, and they were four. We were small, and they were big. They went to school and were special, and we didn't, and we weren't. It was the circle of life for kids all over the world, I'll bet. But I no longer cared about circles or life or the world as, a whole year of endurance had come to an end at last, and I was finally going to school.

As I walked to school with my Mum for the first and only time, I started to feel self conscious. "Will I like my classmates? Will they like me? Will I like school dinners?" These were the kinds of thoughts that raced through my mind. I hadn't slept much the night before because I was so excited, and I kept getting up to touch the clothes that were laid out at the bottom of my bed. They were new and included new socks and shoes. Never had I had so much new, bought just for me. Usually, I got the stuff that Sandra outgrew, and when I outgrew it, it would go to my younger sister and maybe on to my brother after that, if possible. But this time was different. Every time I touched my new clothes my heart would dance a little faster, and after a moment, I'd become overwhelmed and excitement would turn to fear. Then, I'd remember all the stuff that Sandra had talked about over the last year, and my fear turned to excitement, which calmed me down.

I must've fallen asleep at some point as I woke up with a poke from my sister, who screamed into my ear that it was time. As I chewed on my toast, I ignored the chaos in the background, with my Mum shouting orders while she bathe and dressed my siblings, and I thought about what it would be like to learn while Tony Blackburn screeched out of the radio. I couldn't wait to meet my new teacher and was so excited that I couldn't finish my bread. I stood by the front door impatiently, willing my mum to hurry up as she settled the kids. Finally, we were on our way. Sandra skipped away in front having met some of her classmates and I tagged along with my mum, suddenly fearful, helping to keep order with the kids. The walk was short as school was situated behind the block of flats where we lived, but it seemed to go on for ages, as I hadn't got the hang of measuring time yet.

The school was a new building, and Mum said that it had been built specially for the kids on the housing estates that had sprung up in our part of Hackney. She said that it didn't follow the usual layout of the older schools, which were stacked up high with playground cages in the roof. Nope. It had lots of playgrounds and was an infants and primary school all rolled into one. The classrooms were really roomy, bright and shiny, with walls with empty pinboards and plenty of space. The Upper school had three playgrounds – a netball cage, a grassed area and a lowered football pitch – which allowed for ball games without breaking classroom windows. It had a main hall and a garden out front and to the side of the school kitchen, with some flowers but mostly vegetables. It felt like it had been designed for kids to feel at home and I felt at ease with the place instantly. I breathed in the smell of newly waxed floors and my fears disappeared.

Mum took me up to the entrance and left me at my classroom door. I didn't look back and neither did she. She knew that I wouldn't have any problem settling in, as I now played school practically every day since I was three, thanks to my sister. I pretty much knew what to expect – or so I thought.

There was a great deal of confusion and upset that morning. Kids were clinging to their parents for dear life. One kid was literally screaming "MUMMY don't leave me, pleassse!" Another parent was trying to unclasp her child from her skirt. His white knuckled grip and her look of desperation told me that she wasn't winning. "A little help here . . ." she asked the teacher who was nearby. Other kids were running around, touching this or breaking that, while some of the mums chatted in the entrance as they tried to keep tabs on their toddlers. I watched it all dispassionately, took a seat in the corner on a beautiful, green and brown reading carpet and waited for school to begin. How can I remember all of this? Well, it was the first time that I noticed that I was different to the other kids.

For me, school held no real fear, only an anticipation of good things to come. As for the other kids? All I saw was terror. Maybe I'm being harsh. What I think I may have seen was that they weren't excited. How could that be? What was wrong with them? Or perhaps I should have asked what was wrong with me? I waited patiently for all the dramas to play themselves out. It was a bit like when my sister threw a strop, you just had to let it play out. Couldn't make it happen quicker than it was meant to happen, or she got real mean. Real quick.

Our teacher sat at the front of her desk and called us all over to the carpet to sit. I'd been sat there for ages, watching, listening and taking it all in. The smell of chalk, new books, paint and the boy's toilet just down the hall. Heaven. While we were waiting for the other kids to quieten down, she had introduced herself. I smiled shyly and told her my name. She asked if I had any questions and I only had one. "Where are the books?" came tumbling out of my mouth.

At last, all the parents finally left, and all my classmates were seated on the carpet in front of our teacher. It was a bit scratchy on the rug, but who cares? I discreetly kept rubbing the back of my legs where it tickled and hoped that nobody would think that I was picking my bum. Miss Challis was a wonderful vision of cheesecloth and perfume. Her flowing dress made her look like she was floating, and her platform shoes were cute. Her legs were really brown for a white lady and her hair was long and browny blonde and tied back with an alice band. She smiled a lot. I mean really smiled, with her green eyes, her teeth, her whole body really. I remember that she looked like an angel to me. Okay, I was four and hadn't seen a real angel – it was just that I hadn't ever seen anyone that looked the way she did. Or smelled the way she did, like summer. She looked beautiful, vibrant and alive. Not burnt out, tired and a little broken, like most mums did.

I hung on her every word and loved every minute of school. I played in water, I played with sand, I played in the dolls corner, briefly, and then I was introduced to the book corner. A whole corner of books. That was it for me, I was hooked. Towards the end of the day, we all sat on the carpet and one by one, Miss Challis asked each child to recount their favourite activity of the day. That was easy for me. When asked, I said that reading books was my best activity.

"You mean looking at the pictures," she corrected gently.

"No, I mean reading books," I said again.

"Well, in time you will read the books," smiled Miss Challis. "And the pictures are there to help. Did you find then helpful when guessing the words?"

I was aware that I wanted to answer truthfully and that my turn was taking too long as I could sense that the other kids wanted their time to speak. I could also sense that Miss Challis wanted to take the time to make sure that I was describing my activity properly. She was still smiling so I tried again.

"I was reading the books, Miss." There was silence. She was pissed. I could tell. It was the kind of silence that happened when you do something wrong, and your mum gives you a chance to confess. More silence. And then she finally moved on to the child sitting next to me. She continued around the class without any stops and amazingly, it was the end of the day. We all ran off with smiles on our faces and our first pictures in tow and I couldn't stop talking as I walked home with my sister. I could tell she wasn't really listening as she kept walking off and cutting into my sentences with totally unrelated stuff, but it didn't matter. School had lived up to my expectations, and more.

After we had dinner and changed out of our school clothes, we went outside to play. I'd hoped that now that I'd started school, that I'd be able to play at being the teacher, but no. My sister and her friends had other ideas. They were five and I was four. They were big and I was small. I was never going to be old enough to be the teacher it would seem.

The next day, as I went to put my cardigan on my very own special peg near the girl's toilets, I heard Miss Challis calling my name. I turned and went over to the carpet where she stood. She knelt down, smiled at me and said quietly that there would be times that she would correct me and that it was all part of the learning process – or words to that effect. I knew straight away that she was talking about what I'd said the previous day, and I just didn't get what the problem was. So, I said it again. "I was reading books Miss." By this time, I was revising my opinion on how nice she was. She was still smiling with her mouth, but not so much with her eyes. I knew I was in trouble, but just couldn't work out why. I started to feel hot and bothered, and was wilting from the unexpected, and unwanted scrutiny. I'd always hated being the centre of attention and this was no exception. She tried another tack.

"Did you have a particular book that you really liked?" she asked. I nodded. She took my hand and asked me to show her. Now this was the kind of attention that I liked – when someone showed an interest in me and what I liked to do. I was pretty starved in this direction being one of many kids, but I'm not complaining as my Mum did the best that she could do. It was weird having an adult focus on me for all the right reasons. The class was still empty so I knew that I would have her all to myself for a little while. Bliss.

We went to the book corner and I pulled out the book that had caught my attention. She opened it and asked me to read it – and I did. Now, I think that she expected me to make up words based on the pictures, but I was accurately, and without hesitation, reading the author's words. I could feel that I must had done something right as I could see that she was once again smiling with her eyes. She picked out another book and asked me to give it a go. That wasn't a problem for me and once again, I started to read. She was astonished! "That's amazing, how long have you been reading?" she asked

"I don't know" I replied.

"Who taught you how to read?" I shrugged and looked around. All of a sudden, I was conscious that the class had started to fill up, and that all eyes were on me and Miss Challis, cosy in the book corner. Some of the mums with their toddlers were still gossiping while looking in my direction. The kids in my class were looking around for our teacher and their eyes settled in my direction. All probably wondering why Miss would want to have a conversation with me – by myself, all alone.

"I don't know" I once again replied. I started to feel uncomfortable and couldn't quite pinpoint why. "Ok, that's enough attention," I thought to myself. It was the first time in my life that anyone had focused on me like that, and it felt weird. Everybody was watching me, and I didn't like it. The mothers, the kids, literally everybody was now looking in the direction of the reading corner – at me. I wouldn't have said that I was a geek or autistic, but maybe just a little awkward, as I did like to keep a low, low profile. So, this is what my thoughts looked like: PRESSURE, PRESSURE, PRESSURE, followed by a dose of STRESS and just a little smidgen of TRAUMA. Thirty kids and their parents looking at me all at once was way too much attention.

And then it happened. I knew it was coming, and my anxiety amplified times ten. It started with a slow trickle out of one nostril and then started to run a little faster. "Oh, my dear!" announced Miss Challis in a startled voice. She jumped up from her crouched position and rushed to her desk to get some tissues.

"Too late," I thought. I knew what was coming next . . . And out it came in a torrent of red, molten heat. Big, heavy globules of blood. They fell in fat droplets, all over the reading corner floor, all over my dress and very slightly over Miss Challis's toes that were poking out of the platform sandals. There was no stopping it. I grabbed a bunch of tissues and wanted to curl up and die.

An ambulance was sent for because the blood decided that it didn't want to stop. People were freaking out and pointing and some of my classmates were actually screaming – loudly. One of the mums had nearly fainted and had to sit down on an undersized chair, and my classmates were various shades of green and were possibly going to throw up. It was ugly. The commotion that followed would have been hilarious, had it not been centred around me. You see, for me this was normal. For them, it was mind-boggling. I'd gotten through a couple of boxes of tissue in a short space of time and the head mistress had been called. She also started to panic at the sight of so much blood, however she must have realised that it was freaking out the parents and children in the class, who were openly ogling and pointing at me as they talked. She ushered me into the medical room to wait for the ambulance. I was overwhelmed and a little bit intimidated, as I was not used to a nosebleed causing such a fuss. And I was not used to being fussed over. My family didn't treat me differently when it happened at home as I'd had so many, that over time, it had become a normal household event. In fact, I hadn't really given any thought to how others might react as, up until then, only my family had seen me in action. As I tried to absorb this new information – that people found me distasteful, unattractive, and ugly – I realised that I was in shock.

Normally, I had no control over when and why my nosebleeds would begin, but on that day, I knew that it was the pressure of that moment that had proved too much for me. I just knew it. To suddenly be the centre of attention for all the wrong reasons? Nobody wants that, especially when you're only four years old. As I started to process the commotion and the reactions, I began to feel ashamed. The thought of everybody seeing something as personal as my nosebleed, made me feel ugly – like I was a freak. In front of Miss Challis, all over her shoes. I remember when her gaze had turned from wonderment to what – surprise, fear, distaste. I couldn't tell.

This was new territory that I hadn't explored before, and I wasn't very happy where it was leading me. I'd never had to consider how I felt about my nosebleeds, as I'd always taken a practical approach to it – my nose bleeds and I sort it out. It was simple. Not so anymore. The reaction of everybody confirmed that I was not normal, disgusting, which had a profound effect on me. The looks on their faces, the pointing, the whispers, the kids screeching "urhhhhg!" I felt exposed and dirty and well, as if I'd done something wrong.

As I thought about it, I realised that I had begun to pick up on the fact that I was a nuisance at home when a nosebleed occurred. It was never said of course, but their reactions were not great. Nothing would stop. No-one asked if they could help, checked on me if I was holed up in the bathroom for awhile, got me tissues when I ran out. Not a very attractive reaction to something that was beyond my control, but that's just the truth of it. I was left to my own devices to sort it out when my nosebleeds occurred. "You know what to do – so get on and do it," was usually what Mum would say. I took the view that Mum had her hands full and so, even though I could barely reach over the bathroom sink unaided, I managed. Most of the incidents were quite small and would be over after fifteen minutes or so. But they were frequent and unexpected, so I was never prepared when they happened. It kept me on edge, jangling around at the back of my mind – always expecting the worse. Plus, there was an underlying feeling that I was an inconvenience, that I was yet another problem that Mum had to deal with – on top of everything else.

I snapped back into the medical room and realised that I'd gone through yet another small box of tissues. "It should've stopped by now," I thought. But on this occasion, it went on and on, and even I began to get frightened. I knew that something was wrong, that this time was different, and the fear the gripped me was unexpected and beyond words. Miss Challis had been sent back to reassure the class and the headmistress was great, hugging me tightly in between handing me tissues. She said, "not to worry if I get messed up dear, I have a change of clothes in my office." That kindness was not expected. I'd never heard of anyone that would allow you to bleed all over their clothes, who walked around with a change of clothes and, . . . all of a sudden, I began to cry. I tried to be brave and matter of fact about it. I tried to be a big girl but, in the end, I was just a kid who was out of her depth. Overwhelmed. My heart was breaking as I'd waited so long for school and now it was ruined. All I could think was that I'd caused a lot of fuss and bother, and I was uncomfortable and deflated. I wanted to make the best impression and it had gone wrong and, and . . . the tears spilled out of my eyes and I cried. Quietly. For all the times that I'd tried to be brave when I'd had a nosebleed at home. I was strong and independent, but mostly I was a scared little kid. I cried for every time that I'd had to cope with it, again and again and again on my own. Now, every-one knew, well, everything, and I felt so ashamed and ugly as I hugged my headmistress tight and didn't make a sound as the tears rolled onto her jacket, along with the mess from my nose.

My sister was called from her classroom and she went home in a police car to tell my Mum that I was at the local hospital. She was well pleased to also be the centre of attention on that day, as she was the first kid among our group to end up in a police car. She wouldn't be the last.

The ride in the ambulance took literally two minutes as the hospital was situated up the road from the school, and around the corner from the flats that I lived in, which was a shame. I glanced around and was amazed that they managed to fit so much in such a small space. I began to calm down and answer the questions that the ambulance team asked. My headmistress came along with me, and I was so grateful, as the thought of being on my own terrified me. At the hospital, they stuffed my nose full of gauze which stopped the blood from coming out, while they stuck a needle in my arm to put back some of the fluid that I'd lost – no doubt from all that crying. I didn't mind the drip but hated the gauzy nose as I ended up swallowing tons of warm, sickly blood on that day. It tasted slightly like metal I noticed, trickling down the back of my throat like molten lava, forming a pool in the pit of my stomach. I thought it should be allowed to flow out, just like it wanted to – but they didn't seem to care about that – didn't seem to care about what I thought or felt. So, I sat still and silent and let them do what they wanted to do. Eventually it slowed and stopped. Luckily, I didn't have to have a blood transfusion, and was allowed to go home the same evening.

As I lay in bed that night, I tried to make sense of all that had happened during the day. I realised that it wasn't normal to have nosebleeds, and that they were not particularly attractive, which in my mind meant that 'I was not particularly attractive'. I realised that it wasn't normal to be able to read at my age. In fact, I had no idea how I could read – I just could. And, by the way, I learnt that that wasn't normal either. I also realised that I felt ashamed, that I wasn't like everyone else, that I had an illness. It was like a dirty secret had been outed. But, I'd survived. What a day!

I remember that I mulled it over and decided, right then, that I was okay with being different. In fact, as I lay in bed, twirling thoughts around in my head, I realised that I quite liked being different – I think. It wasn't as if I had a choice, did I? That night, I made a decision to never feel ashamed of who I was again. Of course, I did feel ashamed again, many times over, but to my four-year-old mind, I only equated feeling ashamed with my illness. I suppose it was at that point that I started to understand myself. A little. And I fell asleep, feeling better about the day.

I was welcomed back at school the next day as, like I said, my Mum had no time for illness, and I couldn't think of anything worse than missing school. I quickly settled down to the business of being in a classroom full of kids, and also being the teacher's pet. I had reading lessons with her to accelerate my learning and eventually also gained access to the school library, as I'd powered through all the books in my classroom. I still had nosebleeds while at school which was a pain, but nothing along the scale of the first episode. On the plus side, that incident pretty much guaranteed that I got to go to the medical room any time a nosebleed occurred, with a stack of books under my arm, personally chosen by my teacher, to do what I loved to do most – read.

Fifteen – Back at the party . . .

I could hear Barry White in the background crooning about his 'first, last and everything', and tried not to feel too resentful that my nose had decided to play up and bleed at such a crucial time. "Are you kidding me?" I thought as the blood pulsed into the bath and my head continued to throb. "My first kiss . . ." Once again, the embarrassment enveloped me as I remembered the looks as I'd rushed to the bathroom. When did all those people arrive? I sighed. "Oh my god, his breath was so warm as he leaned down to, to . . ." I was interrupted and brought back down to the party as Earth Wind and Fire hit the turntable with one of my favourites, and the bathroom door began to move.

"I need to wash mi hands," someone shouted through the door. There was a pause and then she tried to edge her way into the way too small bathroom. She stopped suddenly as she probably realised that she couldn't just barge her way in.

"Well, you can't, my nose is bleeding," I replied. The gruffness in my voice was lost on her as understandably, I just wasn't in the mood for company. She tried to pop her hand around the door but felt resistance.

"Cha, girl, I need to sort my hair out – I'm coming in," she announced, pushing hard. As she toppled forward into the room, Sheila pulled herself upright abruptly. "Ewwww," was all she had to say. She didn't wash her hands, nor did she do her hair. She just stared.

It was a small space that didn't really have room for two. I was literally slouched over the bath that I'd cleaned hours earlier, head to one side, leaning on my arm while I squeezed tightly on my nose. The bath was sprayed with blood that had dribbled out onto the white enamel and had pooled around the plughole and beyond. Some parts, darker in places than others, had congealed into jelly, forming an almost solid mound in liquid chaos. Soiled and bloodied tissue lay scattered on the floor. It was an unexpected sight to be greeted with, and Sheila's mouth remained unclosed, even though she hadn't uttered another sound. Her eyes hadn't stopped moving – left to right, left to right, and I could see something more than shock when I glanced up. Fear perhaps?

"Oh my gad gyal! You want mi fi call someone? Who did it? Who did dat to yuh face? That guy yuh was dancing with? Cos 'T' can sort him, yuh know? Bikaaz . . ." Her staccato voice trailed away, as she waited for me to . . . 'just say the word!' She'd lapsed into patois and adopted a karate stance which suggested that she was ready to do battle on my behalf. It became clear that I was going to have to talk her down, before she hurt someone.

"No, no, it's fine" I took my hand off my nose to automatically reinforce my words and the blood started to gush faster. I quickly put it back and squawked in a higher pitch, "it's just a nosebleed. I have them all the time."

"Oooh, oh oh oh," said Sheila "I was just about to get 'T' to deal with tings, yuh know?" I could tell that she was still on high alert.

"Honestly, I've had them since I was a baby," I cooed, voice low, without drama. That seemed to be working.

"Oh, oh oh oh," said Sheila, as she backed out of the bathroom, eyes still moving, quickly.

I heard the door close. I paused for a second, trying to digest the whole exchange. "What just happened . . . and who the hell is 'T'?" That was the only thought that I could come up with. I couldn't help but smile. I'd never really spoken more than a few words with Sheila as she was Sandra's friend. And here she was, ready to fight for me. Crazy!

I looked around the bathroom. It wasn't the most comfortable of rooms being a rectangular shape that didn't really allow for much space beyond the bath and a handbasin, which had a medicine cabinet directly above it. The cabinet mostly housed all my remedies for nosebleeds, fevers and cold sores. None of them worked and all were probably past their sell-by date. I suspected that they made Mum feel as though she was helping. I kept quiet about their uselessness and pretended to be hopeful every time she brought one home. Most came from the Chinese herbalist who also provided slimming teas and herbs that promised to help her hair to grow faster. Neither remedy worked. My mum remained forever chunky, and her hair continued to grow at a steady, if unremarkable rate. Her most useless purchase was a nasty smelling grease which was applied to a cold sore before it became visible to the naked eye. I knew that she meant well but, who applies a remedy before sickness actually occurs?

A handrail housed a couple of new, but dirty towels next to the basin and a basket sat alongside the bath, for our dirty clothes. It was usually full to overflowing but, because of the party, Mum had stashed the wash elsewhere. Earlier, one of my jobs for the day had been to clean the bathroom and toilet. Everything gleamed, new soap, new towels, and the bath and handbasin had been scrubbed with bleach to remove any sign of grubby children and domesticity. "It's all disappeared," I noticed forlornly. "It's such a mess in here." I moved my legs as they started to cramp, but I couldn't do much about it. My leg went taut, and I waited, and waited and then it relaxed. It hurt like hell.

"Maybe I can let go of my nose now" I prayed. It had been around thirty minutes and I was starting to get worried. I hadn't had a nosebleed for this long in ages and it felt alien, almost unreal. "Is this me, is this my life?" I questioned. "I should be someone else – I should be someone that'd just gotten her first kiss!" I cringed at the thought of what should have happened, but didn't.

Initially, people had shown an interest, having watched me race through the crowd, making a beeline for the bathroom. Knocking on the door, they had asked things like, "you alright?" or "do you want toilet paper?" It felt nice that people cared, after all, that's what friends did – they showed support and tried to help. Their interest, however, was momentary. It was a party after all and, maybe I just wasn't that interesting. Those that shuffled in, followed a pattern. First, their eyes would start darting everywhere except on the mess that was me, and then they'd back out sliding along the bathroom wall, positioning themselves closer to the door. There wasn't much room, so it all got a little awkward very quickly as they tried to escape. As soon as a banging tune started blaring out from the speakers in the living room, they made an excuse and left. Maybe not true friends after all.

Time went past and I noticed that it was a really warm evening. Even though the bathroom window was open, "Jeez," I felt hot and also something else. It took awhile to locate the feeling of sadness that came over me. It had been ages since anyone had popped their head around the door and I felt . . . forgotten. I promised that I wouldn't do it anymore but, I just couldn't help it.

Tears ran down my face. They started as a slow trickle and quickly fell hard and fast. Tears began to fall, and wouldn't stop. I couldn't understand what was happening. It wasn't as if I was sick? Was it? I'd gotten so used to dropping out of things at the last minute or being missed out of events so often that, I think I'd become a little blasé about what had happened to me – how it all impacted me. The memories came thick and fast, and I remembered times when I was literally overlooked at home, and at school as I was squirrelled away in a bathroom, willing my nose to stop bleeding. Forever, this had been happening, which meant that I never relaxed, was never sure when it would happen, where it would happen, and what it would stop me from doing. I cried hard. Wishing my life to be normal, uneventful, mundane. I'd never really considered the cost of such an illness, sickness, curse or whatever it was – what's the point? But, on this day, or night as it were, at this time, it hurt like hell, and that was the point. And I cried.

"Let's face it, it happened too dammed often for anyone to care anymore," I thought. I knew the drill and so did the rest of my family. I would be in the middle of everything – playing, watching tv or just chilling and then it would start. The lurch in my stomach would follow as I dashed for some tissue. It was always the same 'stop what you're doing and run to the bathroom' lurch that followed the blood. My insides knotted up and tensed as I willed it to stop sooner rather than later. The headaches, the feeling of being drained and really tired that came after, and sometimes before events. The feeling that all around you had moved on, when I'd gotten things under control and tried to rejoin my life. Sitting out of netball matches when I had been the star of the game fifteen minutes earlier. Missing my turn as I ran upstairs when playing out, stemming the flow, and coming back downstairs to find that I'd been taken out of the game, any game – all the time.

I guess that it became hardwired into my routine, and probably accounted for me playing alone and reading more. I always felt that promise of foreboding and doom, like at the beginning of a horror movie – when you know something bad is gonna happen, but you just can't work out when. I'd just wanted to wish it away, as it stopped me playing 'knock down ginger' or missing the end of the film on the telly. I'd wish for it to be quick, so that I could get it over and done with, not lingering for people to comment or feel sorry for me. Always, I wished that it didn't happen at all.

***

I think back to a time when I was shopping in the market with my Mum, and it started to flow. I was younger, maybe about five, so didn't walk around prepared as I do now that I'm fifteen. I didn't have a tissue and neither did my Mum, so I had to make do with my tee shirt, and use it as a napkin. I covered my nose and squeezed as tight as I could, milling around in what seemed like the busiest market in the world, on that Saturday morning. Ridley Road was hot, crowded, and just too much. It seemed to me that adults always walked with their eyes forward and never down, and if you were nearer to the ground like I was then, you were invisible. I could see lots of women, colourful and loud with their shopping trolleys, shuffling around. I could smell the sweet aroma of overly ripe fruit – too sweet – and the lowkey whiff of rotting meat, and I watched, as they ushered their children in front of them, as they carried the trolley overflow. I walk closely behind my Mum, trusting that she will take me through those people quickly, painlessly. I remember that I could barely see the sky, the buildings, or the pavement. All I saw was the backs of the women who were jostling to get the best of what was on offer.   Back then, the choice must have been limited. No plantain, yam or sweet potatoes. Apples, oranges, tomatoes and bananas all for sale, as each stall holder screamed for attention because of course, his stuff was better than his neighbours. "Cum on ladies, apples, oranges, cum on, you'll never get a better price, look at 'hat, quality mate, quality. Cum on ladies, fresh veg, 'ave sum 'o that, ladies." We were nearly at the middle of the market – I know because the smell of fresh bread started to fill the air. It soothed me and helped to make the market feel like an okay place. I wasn't sure of our direction anymore as Mum stopped, again, to talk to yet another friend. I stood there, guarding the trolley as she talked about 'other people's business'.

"Joyce yuh alright?" Mum asked the same question every time she saw someone, and they always replied with the same answer.

"Yeah man, mi alright," said Joyce. Then they would cut to the chase.

"Mi hear seh dat Brenda is pregnant," Mum would always drop the clanger. "Helps to get a better handle on a conversation," I heard her say once.

"Lord hav mercy" or something to that effect would follow from Joyce, or whoever she was talking with that day. A dramatic pause followed, and voices would be lowered. "But yuh did hear the rest . . .?" People like Joyce would then drop another bombshell and my Mum wouldn't be able to compete. Why? Because she didn't play gossip monger. She always said,

"Yuh see me? Huh, I hav mi own problems, I don't hav time for nobody else's." She didn't court gossip, she just liked to stay in touch. So, she didn't care if someone knew more than her as she unashamedly leaned in for more storytelling. "Wha happen?" she'd asked.

"Well," would be the starting words and then came the look. They all did it – look both sides as if they were about to cross the road, and then they'd speak. "It's not fi Bertram tho," Joyce whispered

"A wha you a seh," my mum would whisper back, glued to the spot, hooked into the story for the next ten minutes.

As I stood still, I half listened and stared at the colours – bright – as the market men showed off their wares, specially laid out to look appealing. Many, many people, pushing and jostling, going around each other, making way for each other, never bumping into each other, all focussed on shopping – and gossiping. And then I got bored. I sighed because this was one of the reasons why Mum would take three hours to shop, every week. As I got older and this weekly ritual continued, I remember thinking that shopping should take about an hour and just be about replenishing food and house stuff. But for Mum, mostly it was about meeting friends and 'catching up'. This would happen every five minutes it seemed and would be interspersed with buying a pound of this, or a dozen that. Mum would prod and poke everything to gauge freshness and would "um" and "ahh" before parting with her money. It was a practice that all the woman employed, no doubt learned from their mothers and their mothers before them. The stall holders would just hold back, bag or paper to the ready, waiting for the choice so they could seal the deal. They were busy, but patient, recognising that it was all part of the ritual of buying and selling, I guess.

Having met yet another friend, Mum settled in to talk. I thought that she would be quick, given my nosebleed, but no. They got right into whatever or whoever they were talking about. After awhile her friend glanced at me and asked "wha happen to she?" My mother turned and looked at me like she just remembered that I was with her and said,

"Um, nutten," and turned back to her friend and they carried on talking for what seem like forever. So, there I stood, in the busiest place in the world holding my nose tightly, swallowing hot blood to the point that I thought that I was going to vomit, feeling like I was unimportant. Feeling small and forgotten. I couldn't make a sound because I was an invisible child. I couldn't make her take notice and help me, because I was an invisible child. I had to wait, and wait and wait. I probably wasn't waiting that long, but that's how it felt. She eventually stopped talking and found the stall that sold toilet roll. She handed me some tissue and made a fuss of cleaning me up, but it was too late, the dye was cast. The feeling of being invisible stayed with me – always.

***

I snapped out of the memory and sighed. "Jeez, that happened over ten years ago, and I recalled it as if it had happened yesterday." I was struck by the thought that I'd remembered – hadn't forgotten, after all that time. That feeling that nosebleeds happened to me, only me, and was my problem and nobody else's. That it was an invisible problem. I was invisible. I was a problem. I dealt with it as a child, put up with it and, as I grew, I learnt to hate it. Hated that this thing, this sickness, or whatever it was, had plagued me. And, here I was, about to experience my first kiss in what sounded like a banging party, and once again, I'm in the bathroom. Suddenly, the real impact of my illness stared back at me.

Don't make a sound, just fit in, don't make a fuss, bleed quietly, don't make problems, don't make a mess, too many hospitals, too many doctors, always the same. "She'll grow out of it," they all said – except I hadn't. When will it happen?

When will it stop?

And I cried.

Hard.

I cried for all the times that I'd had to miss out on things, been ignored and forgotten. All the hurt and anguish of being different, of feeling other, of being invisible. For being stuck in a bathroom, waiting for the blood to stop.

Seven

As I once more drift back in time, I remember that Christmas Day. I was seven years old, and I got up really early to gather under the tree with my siblings. We didn't have the courage to open our presents before Mum woke up, so we just sat there, trying to guess what was in the paper parcels. Just to make it more difficult for us to work out what she'd bought us, she would deliberately leave the names off each present. She called it 'fun'. We called it 'torture'. I mean, we'd sit there and couldn't squeeze, tug or peel paper away from any bundle of joy because we had no idea which present was ours.

We didn't have much in the way of decoration, apart from the tree. Always artificial and always six foot, the tree would take up a corner of the living room. The decorations were stored in a box under a bed for safe keeping, but, they were never kept safe enough as most of them shattered. Shards of baubles would line the bottom of the box and once again Mum would have to go to Woolworths and buy some more. Because of this, over the years we built up a mishmash of decorations which clashed and hurt the eye. But that wasn't the point. As we decorated the tree and wrapped silver strands around gold string, hung purple baubles next to green, it became our bit of art. No fighting or disagreements, just kids trying to make a crappy tree nice. Some elaborate paper chain lantern things were hung from the ceiling in the living room, alongside streamers of varying colours which were stuck unevenly on the walls. They were various shades of blue, green, red and yellow and the overall effect was confused and tacky. It was, however, a beautiful sight as far as we were concerned. We spent hours putting it all up and because we used sticky tape, it usually started to fall down after a couple of days. In the end, we just left the tape on the mantelpiece, as stuff eventually started to fall down after a couple of hours because of the heat in the living room.

On Christmas Eve, Granny would turn up and leave our presents. Dressed in the thickest blanket wraparound coat, and her sensible winter ankle boots, she always managed to look stylish. She'd bring in the cold from outside saying 'helloooooooo' in her own special way, and fill my heart with warmth while she stooped down and said, "where's my hug?" She always demanded a cuddle, and we'd clamber around her, happy to see her. She was like Mary Poppins and Father Christmas all rolled into one. As we literally dragged her ever-present bag away from her, we emptied all the goodies under the tree, and helped ourselves to the Murray mints or nut brittle at the bottom of the bag. She would always bring a loaf of coconut sweetbread, along with some wool and her crochet needle. When she took off her coat, she would reveal an amazing outfit which she made for herself. It was the end of the sixties, a time when people still made their own clothes and when a decent dressmaker could make good money. Because Granny was a piecework machinist by day in those days, and a seamstress by night, she only had time to make clothes for herself and family members. She made beautiful stuff like skirt suits, dresses and coats with tailoring and design that was as good as the clothes on the telly. She knew how to dress (even I noticed it, and I was a kid) and she definitely wasn't like regular mum's and granny's who were round and chunky. She was slim and walked straight, proud, with her shoulders back and just the hint of a wiggle in her stride. She hated slouching and was always telling us to 'pull up our necks', which was the perfect way to get us to stand up straight. Even though she was forever sewing clothes for herself as well as making curtains or bedspreads, she always found time to make us beautiful dresses that we could only wear to church. What a sight we were on Sunday's at St Dominic's, the local Catholic church, in our gorgeous dresses and my brother in shorts and a tiny blazer. I felt like a princess, with my posh outfit, my legs greased and hair neat and tidy for that one moment of the week. We had to change out of those clothes as soon as we got home from church though, and because they were only worn on Sunday's, we grew out of them way too quickly. Granny would do alterations so each dress could be recycled and handed down to either me or my younger sister. Always, Sandra would get a new dress, never a hand-me-down as she was the eldest and tall and thin. I was fine with that as Granny would make each dress feel like it was made 'just for you', whether or not it was a cast off. We had a set of dresses that Granny made out of Mum's wedding dress when we were about three or four. White, with tiny blue flowers, it was one of my favourites which I wore with white ankle socks and my Sunday shoes. It was a part of history that we all had a hand in, and I wore that dress until it looked stupid short on me. Then I wore out Sandra's dress which was just as pretty and made me feel like a bridesmaid, until that became too small. We would grow so fast that Granny was constantly having to make us new clothes, but she didn't mind though as I could tell that she took great pleasure in being able to make us all look our best. She didn't need to fit us, as she just knew our sizes and her eyes would soften when she saw us in our outfits.

Sometimes, she would take me and Sandra out on the weekends as we grew older. We'd put on our dresses and hop on the number seventy-three bus into Oxford Street and go window shopping. We'd walk the length of Oxford Street and gape and gasp at some of the window displays. Filled with ideas on fashion and other ways to spend money, it was like being transported into another world. Marble Arch looked so grand and imposing, surrounded by buses and cars going in all directions. Everyone wore nice clothes in the West End I noticed, and, I also noticed that there were no black people in that part of London, apart from us. That didn't bother Granny one bit, and we would take our time wandering around, looking at carpets, vacuum cleaners, curtains and furniture in the shop front displays in Selfridge's, Harrod's, BHS and Marks and Spencer's. Eventually we would pop into Littlewood's and travel up the escalator and into the cafeteria where we would have fish and chips with a glass of coke. Taking our time over the meal, we talked about what we'd just seen and decided which was our favourite store front. People would look at us just a little too long, not long enough to call it ogling, but long enough to call it staring. I could see it happening out of the corner of my eye. I felt so proud of my Granny that I didn't mind the stares. I felt refined and gentile with my table manners that Granny had taught us. So, I didn't mind that people felt the need to look. I felt so pretty in my dresses that I was glad that they had something good to look at.

We took the seventy-three bus home again and slowly as we travelled through Kings Cross and on to Stoke Newington, I could see the difference in people. Not so upright and well dressed. More and more black people. Streets that became dirty and buildings that looked shabby, welcoming us home. We'd take off our dresses and slowly adjust back to our lives in Hackney. The dresses would hang in the wardrobe, hardly worn, and I would touch them gently from time to time, feeling proud, as if they were medals that I'd won.

When we were really little, Granny would stay over for a day or so, but as we got older, she'd spend a few hours and go back home for Christmas Service at her local church. Many years later, she let on that the noise and commotion of Christmas used to drive her crazy. So, she would let us enjoy the raucousness of the day on our own, and usually turned up on Christmas Eve and Boxing Day. She'd often spend Christmas Day with her friend Ann, who had no family, apart from a sister that she didn't get on with who lived in Ireland. Ann spent many Christmases at our home, and we got to know her really well. She had a head of beautiful silver hair that she styled like the queen, and a huge appetite which belied her slight, almost frail appearance. She loved to eat and never said 'no' to anything that was put in front of her, and always managed to clear her plate first. She was funny and lively but like Granny, she was totally out of her depth after spending a few hours with us noisy, squabbling kids. So, she would turn up on Christmas Eve with Granny, and disappear until next year. Come to think of it, we never got a present from her. Hmmm . . .

Eventually, Mum would wake up and the Christmas Day rituals would begin. She would order us all into the bathroom and, then to get dressed. We always had to hit the bathroom before we could begin the day of Christmas properly in her eyes. We groaned and moaned but knew that this was non-negotiable. We quickly scattered, rushing to get washed and changed so that the next part of the day could begin. I remember thinking that I would burst with excitement some Christmas mornings. My Mum would put her Jim Reeves records on, and the day would begin to the sounds of either him, Johnny Cash, Tammy Wynette or Dolly Parton. She'd sing along to these guys as she cooked breakfast, "D.I.V.O.R.C.E, becomes final today . . ." she'd sing, in a country music twang. Only at Christmas would she fish them out and only during the morning, on Christmas day would they be played. Eventually, she'd come to her senses and the smooth tones of Al Green would hit the turntable followed by Otis Redding and Aretha Franklin. That was my cue to take over as DJ and I would start to play my favourites. We had a gram which had pride of place in a corner of the living room. It had a beautiful rich solid wood encasement with a radio dial running across the top. The music stations were pretty sparse and the only one Mum would listen to was Tony Blackburn's Breakfast show on Radio One, as we got ready for school in the morning. Most other times, she would play her records. The turntable stack could hold about four discs, which it would release automatically, and underneath the turntable, stood the speaker, which threw out a mellow rounded sounding base and a clear resonate treble. It was an amazing machine which helped me to appreciate my Mums massive record collection. I became the resident DJ in our house as I got older, and eventually Mum would relax when I took over, as she saw that I treated her records with care. I never put my fingers directly on the black vinyl. I 'sleeved' records immediately after playing and dusted each record down with the yellow velvet buffer before putting it on the turntable. I never used my fingers to clear the dust and fluff from the needle, instead, I blew gently, just like she taught me.

We took turns and went in the bathroom. Of course, nothing particularly interesting happened in there as we were more focussed on opening our presents than washing. So, we just ran a few taps, waited for a reasonable amount of time to pass, and pretended that we'd washed ourselves from head to toe. Our clothes were already laid out on the bed from the night before and we hurriedly got dressed and scrambled under the tree.

We then got to open our smallest present, which was usually an orange or tangerine. As we munched on the fruit, the other presents would be distributed. It was always things that we needed like vests, socks or pants and occasionally we'd get new outfits or nightclothes. It didn't matter what it was, it was new. It smelt new, it felt new and it wasn't a hand-me-down. This year, we all had an extra surprise gift, which in my case was a set of books. This made it an extraordinarily wonderful day. I didn't wait for the rest of the ritual to finish, and I couldn't have cared less about anybody else's gifts. I found a quiet, wrapping paper free zone, and started to read. I only stopped to change the records before burying my head back into my book. Sandra came over to me, wanting me to admire her new toy and play. I said "no," without even lifting my head. I carried on reading and in my pre-occupation, probably missed a few warning signs that my sister was well pissed off with me. Even my brother's very loud and awful drumming on his new kit didn't penetrate my state of happy bliss. Edith Blyton and the Famous Five had me well and truly hooked.

Over the next few hours, all the wrapping paper was cleared, and we sat and played with our new toys. Calm had descended on the household and Mum was in the kitchen, cooking up wonderful things that smelled like heaven. Suddenly I looked up, and it was time to have dinner. The dining table normally sat against the living room wall. Today, it was placed in the centre of the room. Mum never cooked turkey as she found it dry and difficult, so we'd have capon, a big fat juicy one, with rice and peas, spinach, roast potatoes, macaroni cheese, stuffing and a beautifully rich, smooth gravy. It seemed to me that my Mum was in the kitchen all day, but it was worth it. The table was groaning with goodies and the food smelled delicious. We all sat, and plates were passed around as we all talked over each other and got on with the serious business of eating. Christmas Day was also special for another reason. We all got our own piece of chicken. Usually, a chicken wing could literally be divided between all of us, but not today. Today we got to choose, and I chose a leg. It glided onto my plate and was the most beautiful sight that I'd ever seen (until next year), golden brown and succulent, with juices escaping from underneath the crispy skin. My mouth started to water involuntarily, and I wanted to grab it with both hands and demolish it in an instant. But I stopped myself. I'd waited a whole year for this moment and wasn't about to end it yet. I picked up the leg and put it to one side. My plan was quite simple. I'd eat everything else on my plate and then save my prize for last.

The meal progressed and everything tasted wonderful. How do mums do that? They cook the same food that they normally cook, but somehow make it taste special and magical on Christmas Day. We all sipped our cokes and laughed and joked, with Sandra ribbing me as always, about reading. She did that often, until I scarcely noticed it. It was the same old banter. It usually started with, "think you're better than us," and ended with Mum telling her to leave me alone. Today was no exception other than for once, I wasn't really paying any attention to her, as I was starving and was too busy scoffing dinner.

I glanced up at Sandra and remembered what my teacher once said, "if you're talking, then you're not really thinking. You can't do both at the same time." I watched my sister's mouth opening and closing like a goldfish, not listening to her constant chatter, just watching. It dawned on me that she must be brainless, as she never stopped talking. Or was it, "if you're talking, you can't listen?" Hmmm . . . I brought up an image of Miss Haggis in my mind, but just couldn't remember what she said. I decided that it didn't matter, and that Sandra won hands down, as she didn't stop talking long enough to listen, let alone think! I brought my focus back to the meal and quickly got rid of my brussels sprouts. I shuddered inwardly as no amount of dressing up could make those things taste decent. This year, Mum had cooked then with little bits of bacon, but they still tasted nasty. I moved onto the macaroni cheese, which was one of my favourites. I realised that my plate was nearly empty, and I slowed down. I still had my chicken to look forward to, and I wanted to savour every moment.

We continued eating until there was a knock on the front door and I drew the short straw. Up I got to open the door as quickly as possible, so that I could get back to the serious business of eating. It turned out that it was one of the neighbours who had run out of flour. I asked Mum if she had any she could spare and of course she did. We lived in a time and a place where everyone was always running out of something or other. It mostly happened on Thursday, the day before payday and on Sunday, because lots of families went to the post office on Monday to get social security payments. My Mum always gave what she could, as she was always on the scrounge herself as she tried to make ends meet. But not today. Today we had a table full of wonderful, delicious things to eat and I came back to the table to resume my meal.

The first thing that I noticed was that everyone was snickering and trying to hide their smiles. The younger kids had their hands over their mouths, but Sandra didn't. She was smiling openly, almost laughing. "I hate it when I miss a joke," I thought. I looked down to carry on eating and noticed that my chicken was gone. "Not funny," went through my mind but, I thought I'd play along when all I really wanted to do was get on with eating. "Whose got my chicken?" I smiled. My younger sister couldn't keep in her laughter any longer and, seeing as I was also smiling, everyone thought that it was okay to chuckle out loud. We all laughed and then after a beat I said, "so, whose got my chicken?" Silence. And then more silence that was way too long. It wasn't funny anymore and everybody knew it. I stopped smiling and then I found out that Sandra had eaten it. She sat there, rubbing her tummy, grinning from ear to ear, laughing her head off. I watched her, not talking, not listening, just thinking as everything around me slowed down and my heartbeat sped up, thumping hard. My first thought was to reach over the table and throttle her, in fact I saw myself doing just that in my minds eye. Banging her head against the table or smashing a glass in her face kind of rage was descending. I just wanted to do something bad to her at that moment, just so that she would know how I was feeling. Instead, I sat there motionless, as I realised that I couldn't do a damn thing. I sat there looking down at my plate, thinking awful thoughts and I could feel my frustration building and building.

Mum could see that perhaps it hadn't been such a good idea to prank me and picked up my plate to get me some more chicken. She came back with some slices of breast – which I absolutely hated. I sat there, stewing. I mean, who liked breast for goodness sake? It's always the last piece to go, after everyone has grabbed the legs, the wings and the thighs. It sits there, waiting for someone to ask for seconds, or gets put in the fridge and used up the following day. The mood in the room had changed and all of a sudden everyone felt awkward, and started eating again, silently. I stared at my plate and I just couldn't take a bite as my appetite had disappeared. I glanced up to see Sandra slyly smiling, and I can't describe the kaleidoscope of emotions that unexpectedly shot through me. It was an explosion that left me paralysed with . . . an emotion that I couldn't quite get to grips with. I didn't get what was happening, but I knew that I didn't want anyone to know . . . To see . . . Beyond my seven-year-old armour, because, I was hurt. I couldn't help it, I couldn't hide it, I just hung my head down and silently started to cry. I felt humiliated that she had managed to reduce me to tears, managed to take my joy, especially on Christmas Day. I didn't want to kill the Christmassy mood, so I quickly picked up my napkin to wipe my tears and nose, so that I could soldier on and eat the dreaded chicken breast. And then came a torrent of blood that whooshed into my plate and covered the breast with ruby red, glistening gravy. "Eyouuu," said the little ones.

"Yuk," said Sandra.

"Wha the . . ." said my Mum, as I jumped up to go to the bathroom. As usual.

Once again, I was on my own. As my nosebleed could sometimes go on for awhile, I was pretty much left to my own devices to deal with it. It was straight forward really. I bled, I went to the bathroom and hung over the handbasin for a while – sometimes a long while. It stopped, and life carried on. This particular one however seemed to be going on, and on, and I was getting tired. My head was pounding, and I could feel throbbing at my temples as the blood continued to run out of me. As I stared into nowhere in particular, I felt resigned to spending a huge portion of my life in bathrooms. Hanging over sinks and just, bleeding to death. Not exactly to death, but you know what I mean! I knew the routine by now and had identified that illness, tiredness or strong emotions such as anger, could trigger an event. My sister had also worked it out and would taunt me, to draw first blood. Every time it happened, with or without her help, it made me feel more and more isolated from everything and everyone. And, it felt like it was getting worse. It happened too often and was setting me apart from my brothers and sisters, I could tell. I felt the difference, their indifference. And it hurt me deeply that my illness was viewed as an inconvenience.

Sometimes, when we were about to go out and play, I'd have to turn back because a nosebleed occurred. I could hear the kids asking for me, and Sandra dismissing me, as I ran back upstairs to bleed it out. It was as if my illness wasn't important. As if I wasn't important. "Perhaps she was right," I concluded. I sighed into the basin. "At least I had my books, and I can escape from it all – some of the time."

***

I joined the local library which, as luck would have it, was located literally across the street from where we lived. I could wander over there, unassisted, easily negotiating the zebra crossing directly in front of the building, whenever I wanted to be alone or disappear from my life. I spent as much time as I could there from the age of about five, and struck up a really good relationship with the librarian. She caught my attention as she had beautiful, gleaming, long brown hair that came all the way down to her bottom, which she wore out mostly, pulled back by a headband. Unfortunately, she was also the plainest creature that I had ever seen. With bucked teeth and slightly troubled skin, and a fringe that came down to her eyes, she looked peculiar. But, all was forgiven because of her luxurious head of hair. I'd never seen hair like it before, so long and silken, never tangled or mussed. Her manner and slow smile were so sparkling, and, unlike my usual interactions, she was also thoughtful and gentle. She always made sure that there was a steady supply of material for me to read, even leaving books for me behind the counter on her days off. I never mentioned her to my family, as I didn't think they'd get it. She was my first adult friend, my mentor. It was a real shame that the library didn't open on Christmas Day . . .

***

As I came back into the reality of my highjacked chicken, I found my sense of humour. I sighed and settled down to the idea of a spoiled Christmas Day, chicken breast instead of leg, and having to once again tough it out until the bleeding stopped. I felt a hand on my back, and I raised my eyes to see my Mum, as the blood continued to dribble into the sink, congealing into a mountain and forming a massive clot. I quickly turned on the tap, swishing the mess down the plug hole, embarrassed that she could see the amount of blood that I was losing, and that I couldn't even be bothered to try and tidy it all away.

"Yuh okay?" I could tell that she was a little startled to see so much mess – so much blood.

"Uh huh" I nodded. And realised that I was okay, and that I was over it. The meal, the laughter, no chicken, the sadness. I was over it.

"I put an extra big slice of apple pie in di oven for yuh – okay?" She said, fussing around me. I nodded again and suddenly in that instance, I felt like sunshine, like the happiest girl alive. Why? Because that was the best feeling in the world. My Mum, fussing over me, looking out for me. My Mum, saying sorry to me, with a bigger than average slice of pie.

Nine

I particularly remember this as a great time to be a kid. It was warm, it was the school holidays, and I was as cocky and as sure of myself as only a nine-year-old can be. We were pretty much allowed to run around outside all day, every day, only really coming home for toilet breaks and food. I got along better with Sandra now that we were older, but only marginally. We still shared the same friends, and she had extended our network beyond the courtyard in our flats. We now played with kids all over the estate, at the swing park and sometimes in the jungle of estates that lay beyond where we lived. My Mum said she'd read somewhere that it was a mixture of housing – a labyrinth of houses, low rise flats, maisonettes and high-rise flats. She said that it had been developed to replace the damaged property of the last great war. It was the first real home for most of my friends. The first time that they'd had their own bedrooms, living rooms, kitchens, indoor toilets, a bathroom and their own front door. This came as standard in the new estates and was a million miles away from the prefab housing on Morning Lane, or rooms in the big, draughty, run down houses that we were used to. I remember moving into the estate. It was a huge deal. Way too much space all at once. But we soon got used to it. "That's what immigrants do," my Mum once said, "we adapt."

Our particular flat was in an estate which had seven blocks of twenty flats, spread over five floors, shaped in a giant rectangle. Each block held twenty families, with their own porch area, stairwell and dustbins. Each flat in our block had a red front door and a balcony room that faced directly into a square. "This would allow for mums to hang out washing, and chat," we were told by housing officers. My Mum never did that, the chat, I mean. She thought that was tacky. "Why would yuh wan fi stan up by your window fi shout all yuh business outside fi everybody to hear?" she wondered. Each room was already decorated in different shades of white with flowered wallpaper and vinyl floors and was ready to move into. It was our first 'real home' and we loved it. Mum was so proud of her living paradise. All of a sudden, she could entertain, and she could say things like "yuh better git to yuh room!" Or "move out fi under mi feet!"

The design of the block had around sixty families overlooking the courtyard which had planted flowerbeds, and room for children to play. This was repeated along the rectangular estate with a huge play area in the middle, with garages and dustbin areas. A one-way road circled within the open grounds with a restricted speed limit of five miles per hour. This made up the estate.

Families got along, they made things work and any tensions that existed, were contained. Many families had one parent, women living on social security, and those that had a man around, were normally surviving on low wages. Nobody had cash to flash, everyone had money worries, and most people made it work, helping each other out when the need arose.

Our group of friends ranged from kids aged four to eleven who played well together and like the adults, made it work. There was one kid, Sharon, that had been burned all over her chest as a baby. She walked around with a metal cage supporting her and was in and out of hospital. She spent a lot of her time having skin grafts, having her cage adjusted as she grew, and dealing with infections that she picked up as a result of her condition. She never complained or made a big deal of the fact that she couldn't quite stand up straight and had a slight bump in her back. She was funny, extra smart and we were always swapping books as we were the readers in our group. I never asked her how she ended up all burned and deformed and she never talked about it. It was just how she was, and we accepted her, no questions asked. She came out to play with the rest of us, when she could, and we'd go and visit her at home when she couldn't. We included her in everything that we did.

Most of the time we'd run around the courtyard playing ball games, hide and seek, and riding bikes and scooters – if someone had one. Most kids didn't have a bike, so we all took turns and shared with those that did. I was into playing ball games 'up the wall', chanting songs and throwing the balls over, under and up in the air as we sang. Stepping up and taking over from others while in motion – always on the left–hand side – sliding in smoothly as we sang . . .

Under the brown bush, under the sea, bom, bom, bom,
True love for me, my darling, true love for me.
When we get married, we'll raise a family, so,
A boy for you, and a girl for me
Pom diddly pom, pom, sexy

. . . throw and catch and up and drop, singing about kisses and boys that we loved for the duration of the song. Giggling, laughing and skipping and playing on the swings and slide located on the estate. I played ball games with the boys, and wasn't too shabby at football, giving them a run for their money as I didn't mind getting down and dirty, being that I was a bit of a tomboy. I wasn't a leader, but I could hold my own.

On this day, some of the kids decided that we needed to go a little further afield and meet up with some friends from school who lived in the estate behind ours. So off we went, on yet another adventure, shoving and pushing and talking non-stop, excited to be doing something a little different.

This estate had a different 'feel' to where we lived. It was much smaller for one thing, and the layout of the maisonettes was different, less kid friendly. There were rows of housing, all the same, stretching for at least a million miles along the whole length of the road, or so it seemed. It was the same on the other side of the road. Also, I noticed that there didn't seem to be many kids out, which was odd, as it was the middle of the afternoon and the weather was fine, with blue skies and no hint of a breeze. I was starting to wish that we stayed in our usual block of flats as I was hot as hell and getting a little crabby and flustered. I also needed a drink, as my throat was as dry as the hair on Melissa Kennedy's scalp.

I spotted Patsy who went to the same school as us and it turned out that it was her manor as she lived just a little further down the street. "Hey Patsy, do you wanna play?" I asked. She seemed to be on her own doing nothing in particular.

"No," she replied, "I'm not really allowed to play with you." I hadn't quite got the gist of what she meant. I mean, I couldn't recall ever playing with her before so didn't understand why we were on her 'off-limits' list. There was a long pause, a moment until one of the kids spelt it out to me.

"She can't play with us because we're black." Loretta said this in a matter-of-fact way, as she seemed unsurprised. But it left me confused. I wasn't stupid but, felt as if I hadn't quite understood what she was getting at. I was baffled.

"Why can't you play with black kids?" I asked her and she replied without hesitation.

"My dad says I mustn't play with wogs, cos you're all monkeys and you'll give me fleas."

My mouth dropped open and I stopped in my tracks. I had to think it through. Firstly, I'd never heard of anyone making any distinctions between us kids based on colour before. Why was it a problem? I was sure that I'd seen her playing with black kids all the time in school. Secondly, wogs? apes? fleas? Or should I be thinking secondly, thirdly and fourthly? Or perhaps should I be thinking IS SHE TAKING THE BLOODY PISS???

While all of those thoughts were rummaging around in my brain and encountering nothing but tumbleweed, something strange happened. I think I may have had an out-of-body experience. Without prior warning, and without sending the appropriate signals to my brain, my hand took on a life of its own and connected with a sharp 'twang' with Patsy's plump white cheek. Once. Or was it twice? I couldn't be sure. Perhaps it was three times. Who gives a shit. It could have been ten times for all I cared. She ran off wailing in the direction of her house and we all stopped on the spot, in silence, for the first time ever.

Loretta, who was a little older and wiser than me, looked at me and screamed, "are you crazy girl!" She patted me on the back as she said it and, as the mist of anger cleared, I could see that my mates were impressed. It was probably what they all felt like doing, the slap I mean, and didn't have the bottle to carry it through. That's not to say that they couldn't hold their own in a fight, because they could be downright mean. But this was different. It hadn't been the usual sort of reason to fight. You know – fist in your face, gonna smash your head in – reason to fight. This was a battle of words which, at our age, let's face it, we weren't equipped to deal with.

It became clear to some of the older kids that we needed to get back onto safe ground, so they shuffled us in the direction of our estate, but not quickly enough. Patsy had returned, her face all puffy from crying and dirty from . . . who knows what! Next to her was a monster of a man, in a white vest and braces which were holding up his trousers over his protruding belly. He was solid muscle with meaty arms which were covered in too many dark hairs. Hairs spouted out of the top and side of his vest and his face was dark with whiskers which he hadn't shaved off that day. His hair was slicked back with something oily and he looked mean. Nasty mean.

"Which one was it?" he demanded of Patsy. He had a growl of a voice that boomed out of his barrel chest. He came bounding up to where we were all standing and staring. He paused in front of the group.

"Her," replied Patsy, pointing her grimy finger straight at me.

All of a sudden it was like the parting of the wave's 'whoosh', like in one of my favourite films with Charlton Heston called 'The Ten Commandments'. One minute I was surrounded by a clump of friends, and the next, I was on my own, with groups of kids on either side of me. This was not good. All of a sudden, I remembered, the story of David and Goliath. I was preparing for my Confirmation at the local catholic church, so knew all about the triumphs of the lesser man. I found myself making comparisons, thinking that I wasn't the lesser man David, so to speak, with a slingshot and without a plan. No, I felt like I was less than that. I was in essence, the stone in the slingshot – tiny. I was completely defenceless, lacking an adult to fight my battles for me. At that moment, I needed someone to guide and direct me, to tell me what to do next. I was riveted to the spot. Scared beyond scared, gaping at the humongous creature standing in front of me half naked, in a vest and braces. And there I was. A scrawny nine-year-old girl that had turned into stone. Everyone had literally stopped breathing.

Patsy's dad strode up to me and without hesitation, grabbed me by the scruff of my tee-shirt. He lifted me clean off the floor, calling me a "dirty nigga" and a "troublemaker." In my mind, he was being unfair, as his daughter was the one with the grimy face and the dirty mouth. But I wasn't about to argue the toss. Hell, I knew that if my Mum heard that I was using words like "wog and nigga", she would have slapped me herself. But everybody's different. For him, my being black was enough of a reason to behave as he did. He was furious, he was frothing, and I was frantically looking for a way out, an escape from his clutches. I was big eyed, limp and vacant, looking in on myself while paralysed, like a fly caught in a spider-web – petrified.

It was then that it dawned on me. She was saying what she'd learnt from him. I knew that while I couldn't properly articulate what was playing out in front of me, there was something about the whole situation that was off. He was horrible, and had decided that it was okay to be that way because he didn't like the colour of my skin. "How could that be?" I thought, "it's just skin! So how could that be?" It was as if my mind couldn't process why he would feel that way, and why he was so, so angry. As I looked into his screwed-up face, all I could see was hate so strong that it was like a tattoo on his forehead. I stared into his burning eyes, which were huge pools of anger, that I was drowning in.

My mind went blank, as I processed all these thoughts and feelings at warp speed, in a milli second. And then, my mind rebooted, like a computer after shutdown, as I tried to 'pick sense out of nonsense', as my Granny had taught me. "This wasn't right," I thought. "It wasn't fair. It was . . ." I struggled to find the sense of things, and I couldn't. "It's just plain wrong," was all I could come up with. And suddenly anger came to me in that moment, like nothing that I'd ever felt before. It'd been boiling away because of Patsy's words but now it was overflowing, a hot and unrelenting torrent, about to erupt like a volcano. "How could he do this to me?" I thought. "Okay, I smacked his daughter and that's not cool, but, what the hell, nobody died. How could they start something like this, say things, grab me, hurt me, and get away with it? How . . . how . . . no . . ." My stomach was rolling around and my heart was pumping hard and fast in my chest. Dry mouthed and unable to swallow not a drip drop of spit, I was suspended in mid-air, flapping around like washing on a windy day. "No . . . I've seen this before," I thought. "you grab, and you kick, and you punch because you can. No, no, no," I knew the drill and I knew what was coming.

I'd seen it at home, with my Mum and Dad, so I knew the score. As I was forced to listen and sometimes see the damage that a man can do, I'd made up my mind. Time after time my Mum was beaten in front of us and behind closed doors. Too many times to count. As I watched, screaming and beside myself with helplessness, clawing at my face, dancing from one foot to another in horror, looking at my sister, both of us full of despair and fearful for our mother's life, I knew that I wasn't ever going to let that shit happen to me. I was four, I was five and I was so tiny, but I knew that I just couldn't. I was never going to allow a man to beat me, no matter who they were. I didn't care about size, shape or how I felt about them. All I knew was that it was never gonna happen to me. I couldn't save my Mum I reasoned, but I could save myself.

Before I could stop and think about the repercussions of my actions, I reached up, pulled my arm back as far as it would go – and punched him. I screamed words at him. It was a guttural sound that came from somewhere deep down in my belly. I was beside myself with rage, and as my anger erupted, it released an inner strength and presence that I didn't know that I had. A wall of violence came at him, for every time that I couldn't help my Mum. For every time I felt the fear that my Dad had made me feel. The unfairness and injustice that I'd encountered was so deep that I didn't even know it was there. Until then. His anger and hatred came right at me unlike, anything I'd ever experienced. Forceful and cocky. I didn't like it. I didn't like it at all. And . . . I squashed it. I squashed him

He dropped me like I had the plague but not before I'd had a chance to really go for him. I scratched, kicked and hollered at him in such a frenzy that people started coming out of their houses to see what all the commotion was about. There was blood everywhere and my friends didn't know what to do. I was possessed. The adults who were milling around, were able to sum up the situation immediately. Everybody knew that there were rules that adults were not allowed to break, and randomly hitting children was one of them. They started to circle around to make sure that no more damage came to me. I sat on the floor, heaving and crying, with blood pouring out of my nose. It didn't look good.

Patsy's dad started backing away muttering, "I didn't touch her – honest!" Nobody believed him. I was calming down now and noticed that quite a crowd had gathered. Patsy's dad looked less menacing and more worried, because of the way that the scene was playing out. The hostility was palpable, and the murmurs had started to repeat the racist words that he had spoken to me. His white vest was now covered in blood – my blood. I lay like a crumpled piece of paper, heaped on the floor, all eyes on me. "Too much attention, too much attention," my mind kept repeating, and I could feel myself retreating back into my usual quiet shell. Empty. Spent.

Unknown to me at the time, at the first sign of trouble, my sister had slipped away to call for help. Mum was at work, but she had left us with a neighbour who was fun, baked great pies and talked really loudly. It turned out that when my sister ran back to our flats, she yelled ferociously at the top of her voice in the yard to get our babysitter's attention. She later explained that practically every window in our block opened and the mums and dads all looked out in concern. She told them that I was fighting with a man on the next estate who called me a 'wog' and the windows slammed shut. This was immediately followed by our babysitter coming out to meet her, along with quite a few mums and dads who were also concerned for their kids who were still at the scene of the 'crime'. They literally ran and arrived at the estate, out of breath, expecting the worse. By this time Sandra said that all she could think about was how my Mum was going to react, as she ran to the front of the crowd with the other parents to see what the commotion was.

They were not disappointed. It was pretty clear that my friends were glad to see the grown ups as they were out of their depth, staring at something unbelievable. They quickly filled them in on what had happened. Our babysitter sat next to me and checked me over to see where I was hurt. Out of the corner of my eye I could see that some of the men had started to advance towards Patsy's dad. The people who had gathered around were black, white, mixed race and asian and were firstly, not impressed that an adult would consider harming a child and secondly, that he was also a racist. I could tell by the way that they were acting and the sympathetic looks that they gave me, that they were on my side. They were all in agreement that it definitely wasn't okay for people to be disrespectful in that way, especially to a child.

As for me? I was clear in my mind that people shouldn't be allowed to hit each other in the way that a man would beat a woman. I'd never been hit by my Dad, but that didn't mean that I didn't feel the blows of my Mum, that I hadn't been battered too. I'd had time to work it through and get that straight from since I was four years old. And even though he wasn't around, and it didn't happen anymore, it was still raw and burnt into my nine-year-old brain. So, I was clear as day on that front. But, this was something else. I didn't know that people like Patsy's dad existed, as I hadn't come across such a thing as race hate. All I knew deep down in my gut was that it was wrong, he was wrong. I felt it with a certainty that was undeniable.

I could hear a siren in the distance and was surprised that the police had been called to the scene. In retrospect, it was definitely a good thing that they turned up when they did, as I feared for Patsy's dad on that day. There were a couple of policemen in the car, and they took one look at me and immediately the older of the two got on the radio and asked for an ambulance to come to the 'scene'. He came and knelt beside me and he instructed the younger officer to round up Patsy's dad, just as another police car arrived. Out jumped two more officers and they immediately started moving the crowd back, which by this time had become quite big. One of the officers asked for statements from anyone who had witnessed the incident, and the crowd size shrunk – just like that! Doors were slammed shut on the estate and people drifted away, as most people wanted nothing to do with the police.

The older officer asked if I was hurting and if there were any marks on me that he couldn't see because of my clothes. He was very calm and gentle and seemed to understand my distress, speaking in a low voice and looking at me with compassion in his eyes. I pointed to my neck which was now bruised raw where Patsy's dad had grabbed me. He put his hand on my shoulders and, even though it was the size of a bear's paw, it was as gentle as the breeze on that summer's day. I flinched a little at first, tensing at the touch of another man, another white man, but he kept his hand reassuringly in place and the tears started to fall again. He didn't speak. He just let me cry it out. He handed me some gauze from his first aid kit to help with my bleeding and as I calmed down, we waited.

Meanwhile, Patsy's dad could be heard in the background, talking to the other police officer in a voice that was just a little too loud. "I'm just talking the truth, aren't I, they're animals. Look what the little monkey's done to my face!" He was being ushered into a police car by the officers, complaining that much to his disgust, nobody seemed to be really sympathetic to his injuries. I could hear one of the officers' explaining that his 'injuries' would be dealt with once they had a chance to take a statement from him. I couldn't quite hear what was being said after that but picked up the gist of the exchange. Since none of the injuries made by a 'nine-year-old girl' were life threatening, he was being advised to shut his mouth and get in the car – before he found himself with a few more injuries to contend with. I couldn't look at him again, but I heard his voice, whining in the background, without bass, without weight. My sister later told me that he was practically shoved in the car and that there was some bruising and swelling around his jaw, as well as loads of scratching on his face. He had bite marks along one arm, and he walked to the car with a slight limp because of the kicking that I'd given him in the shins. I couldn't believe the extent of injuries she described because I couldn't really remember what I'd done. It was beyond weird.

I was being given useless advice by our babysitter on how to stem the blood that was coming from my nose. I could tell that she meant well, but I wished that she would stop fussing and shut up. I mean, it was clear to me that it wasn't going to stop anytime soon as I was just too uptight. It felt like things were still in full-flight and I was absolutely petrified, wondering what the police were going to do to me. It still wasn't clear why the police had been called, and I had assumed that it was because I'd done something wrong. It was as if I was about to be punished for getting so angry, for losing the plot, letting everything out like that. So, I remained scared and waited to be arrested. As I sat with the police officer who had let me cry, I eventually plucked up enough courage to ask in a whisper and with a hiccup "Are you going to arrest me?"

"Am I going to what?" He hadn't heard me, so he put his ear closer to my face to hear. The babysitter however had heard what I said, and she looked up sharply, as though she hadn't considered that possibility. She then altered her position so that she now sat firmly between me and the officer. He clocked the move and smiled.

"No no love," he held his hands up as he said that, like when the police ask the baddies to 'stick 'em up!' in the movies.

"Then what are we waiting for?" I asked, tired, now that the adrenaline was waning, and my nose bleed was still going strong.

"We're just waiting for the ambulance. You've lost a lot of blood and they'll need to have a look at your neck." He scrutinised it again, head cocked to one side, and added, "It looks bad". He caught my worried look and the nods that the babysitter was throwing his way, and finished with, "but I'm sure it's fine." He gave me a reassuring pat on the leg and surprisingly, I was reassured. I could tell that nothing bad was going to happen to me because he would look after me. He just felt like he was that kind of guy.

When the ambulance arrived, the officer escorted me to the hospital where I had a transfusion. They treated my neck, and he questioned me thoroughly so that he could understand what had actually taken place, taking his time while taking my statement. When I was released from the hospital the following morning, he was there to take me home. To be honest, we lived about five minutes away from the hospital, but it was the thought that counts. He helped me out of the car and all the curtains in the block twitched, as he and my Mum helped me walk to our first floor flat.

Never would I have thought that such an extraordinary event would have taken place. I'd no idea what had come over me, but in that moment, on that day, I'd become a hero. The story was told over and over so that, by the time my Mum came home from work, Chinese whispers had started to take effect and the tale had morph into ridiculous fantasy. Instead of fighting one man, I had beaten up three men and a dog, and the police had been called to restrain me and not to calm the situation down. Of course, all of this was lost on me because people were talking 'about' me and not 'to' me, until one day one of the mums from a different block pointed me out to another lady, and they came over and told me that they were proud of me. At first, I thought that they were coming to tell me off, and then I stared blankly at them when they told me how proud they were. I missed a beat, and then the penny dropped. It was the first time that I had been openly praised for anything, so I sheepishly muttered that it was "nothing" and scuttled home. But I got used to it and became more gracious when praised. I didn't mind at first, it was novel that the whole world seemed to be proud of me. For the first time ever, all eyes were on me and I was literally the centre of attention - in a good way. I must admit though that, after awhile, I really didn't like it much. As the chatter about the incident continued, more and more attention came my way and I knew that I was never going to get used to being in the spotlight.

I made a statement at the local police station and had to talk to some very uptight looking adults about what happened. Initially, I was nervous, worried that they wouldn't believe me as

I was only a child, but I was wrong. It became clear that the police were taking both me, and the incident, very seriously and I was able to relax when I saw that the officer from that day was also present. As they described it, "self preservation kicked in, and the rest was a very human reaction to a really bad situation." I remember the words because the officer, kept saying the same thing over and over as I cried and cried when he first met me.

I can't really remember what happened to Patsy's dad, but I'm sure it wasn't good. He was prosecuted and luckily, I didn't have to attend the court bit. Patsy never came back to school after the summer holidays and her family suddenly found it difficult to live in the area. So, they were moved – to Essex.

Thankfully, things went back to normal after awhile, and I was able to disappear into my shell once more. But I was never quite the same. I'd had a rude awakening into violence and racism. And even though on that beautiful summers afternoon my innocence was lost, I found my voice, my courage, myself on that day.

Twelve

I suddenly became aware that most of the things that I was remembering either centred around illness or violence. Not all of my memories go off on that tangent, but mostly, that seemed to be the kind of stories that stuck in my mind. When I think back to my early years, I saw myself as a sickly child, who was pretty quiet, and mostly kept herself to herself. But, I was always drawing attention to myself through illness, and I resented it, as did my siblings – I'm sure. For instance, I had all the usual ailments such as measles, mumps and chickenpox, but I'd have them longer and be sicker than everybody else. I was always, always catching colds, followed by a raging fever, which would then result in endless nosebleeds. That was the usual pattern for years.

Things got a whole lot more interesting as I aged, as I found that periods of sickness would leave me with a cold sore on my lip. Now, I'm not talking about a little something that would develop and was mildly noticeable. Oh no. I'm talking about a massive cluster that would appear in an instant, grow in an afternoon, and take over half my mouth in a day. Herpes virus was my curse. It would normally start with a tingle on the corner of my lip, telling me that something was up. Then out would pop a small spot which looked like a blister a few hours later. Another blister would appear later on, and then another, and then another until by the end of the day, a cluster of eight or so blisters would be grouped at the side of my mouth. My lips would be pink and swollen and looked like I'd been punched on the jaw a few times. I could see people staring as they talked to me, watching as it seemed to throb away and continue to grow beyond what could be considered decent and acceptable. During this stage, it would vibrate, beating its own melody, growing at an alarming rate. I would literally feel it moving, growing just under the surface of the skin . . . and then it would gently fan out onto my lips. Later, as the blisters popped and began to dry out, the swelling would go down on my lip and a rough crust would form, to protect the skin as it began the business of healing. That was a slow and tortured process which looked, in its own way, as disgusting as the early stages of my cold sore hell. The attention that the whole strung out process drew was . . . overwhelming. Let's face it, who wants that kind of attention. Also, if I was honest, I was definitely not okay with being stared at or noticed because of yet another physical oddity that was mine and mine alone. There was nobody that I knew that had them and once again, I was left with the feeling that I was a freak. It was a really horrible time and, what made it worse, was that my family didn't see it as a problem. It just wasn't really taken seriously, nor was I, once again. There were two reasons for this. It wasn't as if I was about to die or lose a limb because of it. And, it caused much laughter and I was the butt of many jokes, as it looked so dammed ugly.

That's the sanitised version of what took place every three months or so for as long as I can remember. My Mum took it seriously to a degree, as she'd buy a small bottle of iodine which she'd slap on my mouth as soon as the blister started to appear, to dry the whole thing out. There were two things wrong with this course of action. Firstly, it didn't work. My cold sores took their sweet time while going through their ugly cycle of blemishing and would not be hurried along by iodine or anything else. The second, was that iodine is purple. Neither of these issues mattered much as I went through the rough and tumble of being a kid. But, as I stepped into the arena of being an adolescent, it became a big problem. Why? Well, because cold sores looked nasty – and, during puberty? You've got to be kidding me. Bubble shaped blisters on my puffy, crusty lips, and on top of that, purple painted iodine? Something had to be done.

I went to see Dr Patel on my own when I was around twelve years old. He was the only Asian person that I knew – apart from

Pamela Chang whose parents ran the local Chinese takeaway. He was from India I think, and he was small, round, and slightly balding. I'd noticed his patchy hair from my many visits to his surgery over the years, as he'd spend more time looking down, writing a prescription, than looking up at us. My Mum and I would sit there silently at our visits year after year, and I would watch his head become less hairy, as he scribbled away in his writing that only he and the chemist could read. He also wore a short sleeve shirt and tie that was totally out of place in his dingy overcrowded high street surgery and the smell of curry constantly oozed out of his skin and breath.

The surgery was located across the road from our estate, next to a chemist with too many products and not enough space on one side, and the launderette where all the cool kids hung in the winter to keep warm on the other. Dr Patel was the only GP in the area which meant that visiting the surgery was a monumental event. People had to wait literally hours for their appointment. His morning session went on until after lunch, even though it was supposed to finish at eleven, and the evening sessions took even longer. Sometimes I'd sit and watch as some of the mums would come in with an army of kids, register at reception and leave, leaving their eldest to 'save their seat'. They'd then disappear, make dinner, and come back for their appointment. Nobody complained or moaned, but I could sense that some people weren't happy about it. My Mum was one of those who thought that it wasn't fair, but she never complained out loud, as she wasn't the complaining type.

It was mostly women who visited the doctor, apart from a few really old bent over men who constantly smoked, wore flat caps and had grey faces. Most of these women came to the surgery with their children, and all of them, had that tiredness that's particular to women with children. Sometimes when I was younger, I'd recognise some of the kids who came in with their mums, and that made the time go quicker as we'd go outside to play. But often, I wouldn't know a soul and would sit there, wiggling in my seat, waiting for my turn.

This day was no different except that I was older, and for the first time, I was on my own. As usual, I had time to survey the surgery. The waiting room was filled with a mishmash of wooden chairs in various states of disrepair, lined up against the wall and in rows. On the oval table, were torn copies of magazines which were hopelessly out of date. The walls had faded posters stuck up with tape – not quite straight – hiding grubby wallpaper while exposing the need for a lick of paint on the walls, doors, and ceiling. I was nervous as I sat quietly, waiting for my turn to see the doctor, which actually felt like forever. I sat there with mums and their babies, old women and more mums and their babies, all with their prams and shopping, in the tiny, hot, sour smelling, waiting room. I sat there with my nose buried in a book, while I waited to see Dr Patel

In a partitioned area, sat the receptionist, who looked up every time the door opened. She had big hair that was straw coloured and looked like a haystack, wore too much make up and shouted a lot. She'd been at the surgery for ever and knew how to keep order as people started moaning about the wait time, queried who came in first, and questioned who should go in next. She would fix people with a hard arse stare full of mascara and eyeliner, without blinking, and order them to sit back down or get the hell out. It always worked. The regulars didn't try it on with her anymore, so it was always great entertainment when a newbie turned up, made a fuss, and got on her nerves. She'd shut them down so quickly that they wouldn't know what hit them, as they found themselves doing the walk of shame back to their chairs with their heads bowed down low. A little bit of drama always helped to pass the time.

The front door opened, and the receptionist looked up at the couple that came in. I glanced in the direction of the door and stared. In came a girl who was a year or so older than Sandra, with her mum, a pram and a baby – her baby. Now, I hadn't seen Jennie around forever but didn't think anything of it as she didn't go to my school, and it had only just started to get warm enough to hang around outside after school and at weekends. But a baby! Now I understood the snatches of conversation that I had heard about her "being up the duff". I pretended to know what that meant when it came up, nodding and snickering along with everyone else, but I didn't have a clue. It wasn't covered in Wuthering Heights or Great Expectations, and it certainly hadn't happened in Jane Austen's books, so I remained in the dark. But now I understood. It all slipped into place. All the laughing and side comments meant that she was pregnant.

And then my mind made a quantum leap. That meant that she must have had sex. "Whoa, slow down!" my mind said. "That's disgusting as she's only a kid – isn't she?" For a moment I remember thinking about what it would be like if that happened to me, and I couldn't even finish the thought. Without a doubt, my Mum would kill me and then when she calmed down, she would probably kill me all over again. This was the worst thing that a girl could do to herself and as soon as I started my period, my mum drummed into both mine and Sandra's heads again and again and again, "don't bother with dem boys dem, they will talk nice eena your ear while they make their way into your fanny."

"MUM!" We would both shout together, embarrassed beyond words. I didn't have to look at Sandra to know that she was cringing as much as I was.

"Wha! Don't 'mum' me, I don't care if yuh a lickle uneasy," she'd say. "It's better than being a lickle pregnant. Mi nah ready fi be no granmutha and yuh two sure as hell nah ready fi hav babies. Huh." She'd then look at us both, hard, to convince us that she was right. She was of course, and even though I didn't fully understand what it took to get pregnant, and what it would mean if it happened to me, I dismissed the whole thing from my mind. I knew it was a no go for me as I was scared witless of boys and emotions and doubted that I'd have a boyfriend. Ever. Also, as I went to an all-girl's grammar school, the chances of me even meeting a boy was slim, if not impossible. I pretty much had it covered, I thought. The same however could not be said for Jennie. As I struggled to get over the shock of it, I watched as she entered the surgery and made a mental note to tell Sandra all the details of this juicy bit of gossip later.

She looked pale and exhausted and she shuffled along next to her mum who glared around the waiting room, as if she was expecting someone to shout out her shame. She pushed her daughter towards the chairs and approached the receptionist to let her know their names. I kept my eyes down on my book but couldn't resist shooting another look at Jennie as she sat down. She looked familiar, but different.

She'd put on tons of weight and her face had a pissed off look, that wasn't there before. She'd morphed into a slightly smaller version of her mum; saggy, angry, with frown lines etched into her forehead and black marks under her eyes. She looked shattered like she hadn't slept in forever. She had been an okay looking girl but that was all gone. She was no longer the belle of the ball, but looked instead like one of the ugly sisters. I could hear her mum telling the receptionist that they were registering the baby as her daughter had just returned from an extended visit to her sister in Ireland – on 'family business'. The mum looked around again, almost daring anyone in the waiting room to contradict her. Of course, no-one did, and she carried on with the business of form filling.

The baby started to whimper, and Jennie whipped it out of the pram, and popped it on her breast to feed like a pro. I stared at the bold veins that ran through her massive orb-shaped boob. I'd never seen anyone breastfeeding before, nor had I ever seen a white breast, and I was fascinated. The baby guzzled noisily and seemed to be poking and fighting, as it squeezed and pulled at the source of the milk. Jennie didn't seem to mind that the baby was playing tug-o-war, its chubby little fists kneading away like a baker making bread. As I watched, out popped the other one and she skilfully changed sides so that the baby could continue to feed. She looked relaxed and at ease with the whole thing, as though she was a expert, and not a fourteen year old spotty faced school kid. She looked up unexpectedly and caught me openly studying her. Instead of covering up her exposed breast a little, she stared back at me in defiance. I looked down quickly and dug deeper into my book, willing Stephen Kings' novel to transport me away from my embarrassment.

At that moment, the receptionist called my name and motioned for me to go into the doctor's room. "Thank God," was in my mind as I scuttled pass the other patients and quickly made my way to Dr Patel. I hit my toe on one of the prams in the small hallway and found myself almost hopping into the room. He didn't seem to notice. He was busy writing – probably automatically writing my prescription.

His room was small and airless with a massive desk against the wall. A dark, worn examination couch occupied the opposite wall, with a poster of a multiple armed woman with a crown on, displayed above. A grimy, opaque window was located on the other wall which had filing cabinets stored in front of it, stuffed with folders and records. A sink was located next to one of the filing cabinets – it was miraculously clean. It occurred to me that I actually hated his little room and I hated coming to see him. I couldn't quite find the words, but there was something about him that was, well, off. In my mind, doctors were saviours, people that wanted to help you, make you well and be supportive while you were ill. But what can you do? There was no choice, only him.

I squeezed myself into a rickety chair next to the desk, and after a little prompting, began to talk. Why was I there? "Well, where to start – so many reasons. Basically, it was about my nosebleeds, fevers and cold sores. They were out of control. I was constantly ill and forever missing school. I was always asking to be excused during lessons to go to the toilets to mop up my blood. And then, there were the cold sores that never seemed to want to leave my lips. I mean, I was wearing so much iodine that it had become my lipstick of choice and . . ." On and on I went, and then I paused for breath. I gulped down some air and then I carried on, and he listened intently while trying not to stare at the blisters and crusts around my mouth. I'd really had enough of my life and I was not very far off from bursting into tears. He "urm'd" and "ahh'd" at the appropriate moment as I talked, and I really thought that I'd gotten through to him, that for the first time, he was listening to me. He cleared his throat.

"Ok, so now, you must please take of your top" he said, fingering his stethoscope which I suddenly noticed was around his neck. I didn't immediately respond as I was lost in my misery and was waiting for a magic pill or miracle to occur. "Come, come, take off your top so I can listen to your chest" he repeated impatiently.

"Wait what?" I thought. "Oh right, err . . . okay", I said. This wasn't how he usually dealt with things when I came with my Mum, and it wasn't what I expected. I was a self-conscious kid that didn't allow anyone in my family to see my body. And now, here I was in an office with a stranger, being asked to show myself. I cringed on the inside, as I really didn't want to do it. I'd just started to grow in the chest department and one side was slightly bigger than the other. As I considered it even more, I realised that it wasn't just that my bits were lopsided. I looked at the fat, balding man, who had sweat stains under his armpits, and I realised that I didn't want to lift up my tee shirt and show him or anyone my body. It was private. My secret. I knew he was waiting for me to move, but I couldn't as I was paralysed with fear, shame and something else.

He was leaning forward slightly, stethoscope in his hand primed and ready to examine me but . . . what? I didn't want to say no to him because I wasn't sure that I could. He was my doctor, and he was in charge. Wasn't he? But it just didn't feel right, and I felt trapped. I wanted to burst into tears, I wanted to leave his room, but most of all, I wanted my Mum. She would have known what to do, how to handle him. But I didn't, so I just sat there.

As I stared down at my hands, it came to me that I was incredibly tiny, and he was humongous. And because I was small and alone, I realised that I didn't really have any choices. It was a feeling that I'd never before experienced, and it grew in my tummy, causing me to breathe faster as I looked up at the door that was closed. I noticed that he was drumming his fingers on his desk, which sounded really loud, nearly as loud as my heart, which was booming in my chest. Bang, bang, bang, beat my heart like shots out of a gun, as I stared at his cluttered desk with dust and paper everywhere. My fear grew and my eyes frantically searched for something to focus on, anything but him. "Come, come now . . ." he looked at my notes on his desk and said my name impatiently. ". . .come, I haven't got all day. I am a very busy man."

"This is not meant to happen," I told myself. "Please just write a prescription so I can get out of here," I thought, and wanted to say.

"I really don't like. . .don't want to," is what I ended up saying, in a tiny voice that couldn't possibly be heard, eyes down as I pulled up my top and vest and a tear rolled down my cheek. "Suck it up girl, suck it up – you can do this," I said to myself as another tear fell on my hand. I stiffened as he leaned forward even more in his seat and a whoosh of body stink hit my nostrils. With his stethoscope in one hand, he put his other hand under my elbow to guide me to stand up. He flipped me around and listened to my back, then my chest, and then my back. He then wrapped his stethoscope round his neck in one fluid movement and then felt my back. His hands were clammy. He flipped me around and felt my chest with podgy fingers, and slowly squeezed my breasts . . . and released, casually touching my bum as his hand dropped.

"Okay, so now you can put your clothes down. Good," he said as he cleared his throat. He washed his hands and wiped his sweaty face, while I lowered my top and wiped away my tears. "Everything seems to be in order," he said as he threw the paper towel into the bin. As we both sat down at his desk again, he explained that while it was a difficult time for me, there was nothing he could do. I remember pausing at that moment. I froze. I'd become hopeful that things had changed because of his examination, that something different was about to happen. But no.

"You will grow out of it" he said in his sing song accent. That was his mantra. Every time my Mum took me to see him about anything, he'd say "you will grow out of it." He had stopped looking at me by this time, and was writing something in my records. I was being dismissed.

"But what about the examination?" I asked quietly. He looked at me blankly. I looked back at him bewildered and irritated by his vacant expression, and total lack of interest.

"Ohhhh, Oh that? What about it?" he asked as he carried on writing. It was then that it hit me. The feeling that I couldn't put my finger on. It was hopelessness. I realised that there was something not right about the way that he'd groped my skinny little twelve-year-old body, because he could. I also realised that there wasn't a damn thing that I could do about it. He carried on writing while I processed these thoughts, while I watched the bald spot on his head which had become bigger, I noticed, since my last visit. I could feel my frustration starting to well up along with the familiar throbbing at the side of my temple. A numbness started to penetrate across my body, rising like a wave, from my chest, spreading up towards my throat, and nestling behind my eyes like a dam about to burst. And . . . I stood up abruptly as I decided that it was time to leave, before I had a nosebleed, or something worse happened. I ran out of the surgery like a frightened animal with tears running down my cheeks as fast as I could brush them away.

Something wrong had happened in that room and I knew that I couldn't tell my Mum. I couldn't work out why, but I just knew that I wouldn't tell her. After leaving the surgery I quickly walked towards the back entrance into the estate, just to make sure that I didn't bump into anyone that I knew, and ended up in the play park, on my favourite swing. Back and forth I went, higher and higher as I cried, my head feeling like it was about to explode, the throbbing at the side of my temple unbearable and then, I stopped. It stopped. I slowed the swing, and I wiped my face. I couldn't tell anyone about it because I was ashamed that I'd let it happen. Didn't put up a fight, didn't say no – I'd just let it happen. I tried to work out why I hadn't slapped him or told him to piss off. I knew I was a gutsy kid, usually. "Maybe it was because you were caught off guard," I consoled myself. "Or maybe," I thought, "it's just what happens, it's no big deal and you're making a fuss for no good reason, as usual." The truth of those words weighed heavily on me as I dragged myself off the swing and slowly made my way home, feeling miserable as sin.

I went straight to my room and the tears started to fall again, which always helped to ease the pressure that was building behind my eyes. This time though, there was no relief. Instead, I kept playing the scene in the doctor's surgery over and over again . . . listen to my back, chest, feel my back, my chest, squeeze my breasts . . . and release.

My sister came in and I became all watery eyed again. I tried to hide my blotchy, swollen face unsuccessfully. As I wasn't really one for sharing my feelings, when she asked what was up with me, I managed to sniffle out that I'd just been to the doctors. I didn't get any further.

"Ohhhh," said my sister knowingly. "You've had your first grope with old Patel? Don't worry about it," she continued, as I stared at her open mouthed. "He does it to all the girls."

I didn't say anything as I'd been literally shocked into silence. She must have taken this as a sign that she should continue. "I think I was your age when he done it to me. Or maybe I was younger," she corrected herself. She paused and had a little think and decided that it didn't matter. So she continued.

"Anyway, I was just as freaked out as you." My look must have indicated that I didn't believe that she could be freaked out about anything, so she nodded a few times. "Yep, luckily Dawn from upstairs told me all about him, cos he did it to her when she was about ten. Remember she had massive boobies really early." I thought back to Dawn and her melon breasts and had to admit that I couldn't think of a time when she didn't have them, even though she was only a few years older than me. "Jesus, at

124

least I had Sandra to talk it over with," I thought. I absently wondered how Dawn dealt with it, as there was only her dad and her brother in her family. I'd stopped crying by this time and wondered if this was normal? Or was Dr Patel out of order, just a dirty old man who liked groping kids. Boys groping girls I could get my head around, because that's what boys do. But grown-ups touching kids? That just wasn't meant to happen. Was it? I didn't have a name for stuff like that. The best that I could come up with was that he was just NASTY!

That night, my mind continued to run over what had happened at the surgery. I didn't tell my mum because, well, I just didn't. She had enough on her plate and also, I don't think she would have got the whole injustice thing that I was feeling. Like my sister, she would have probably said that I would just have to put up with it, put it behind me, and laugh it off. That's what Sandra and Dawn did. But I couldn't. That wasn't me. "But what could I do about it?" I thought as I twisted about in my bed unable to sleep. I tried to distract myself by counting how long I could hold my breath. Thirteen, fourteen, fifteen . . . I let out a huge sigh as I realised that it wasn't working and decided to count sheep instead. Quite a while later, I was still counting . . . one thousand and thirty-four, thirty-five, thirty-six . . . my eyes were aching from being scrunched together too tightly for too long and I gave it up, as I knew that sleep wasn't coming anytime soon. Once again, I became frustrated, but, probably out of sheer boredom, I finally fell asleep with no clear answer to any of my problems.

A few days later I visited my Granny. I loved going to her tiny flat as it was filled with all the stuff that made her who she was. There was an old-style Singer sewing machine which sat in a honey-coloured fold down cabinet which she shined regularly, so that it looked pristine all the time. She was a seamstress who made all her own clothes and most of mine until I was in my early teens. I'm not talking about the stuff that we would run around in on a daily basis, but dresses and skirt suits that we wore when we were going out. Somewhere special, like the Trinidad and Tobago Association dance, or the posh event at the Commonwealth Institute that happened every year. She also went to the Queens' Garden Party quite a few times, but we didn't manage to get an invite to that – "that's only for the 'oldies'," she would say. The hum of the machine was always in the background when I visited, constant and muted, quite distinct and familiar, ever present throughout my life. She had style and flair and the dresses that she made were amazing. They made me breathe in sharply with surprise when I saw them. Always, I would react because each dress was like a work of art. They looked expensive and were the most elegant, flowing dresses that fit like a glove, fit for a queen. Dresses that fell to the floor in colours that showed off her beautiful glowing skin. She had a figure that was made for fitted clothes, with shoulders that were ram rod straight, as if the hanger was being worn underneath her dresses and suits. Upright, is how I would describe her, in a class of her own. I wouldn't go as far as to say that she was snobby, but maybe that she was particular about who, and what she had around her. Nothing about my Granny was by chance or by accident. She was our loving but firm head of the family, and we all looked up to her, were slightly in awe of her.

She was straight and to the point, not cute and cuddly like other grannies on the telly, because she was well, straight. "That's my discipline that kept me moving," she'd say. "I would keep my head straight, focused, and jus had to keep on moving forward. No wobbling, no 'I can't make up my mind'. Things were either right or wrong – no in-betweens," she used to say.

She would butt heads with my Mum, who said that my Granny was hard as nails when she was growing up. That she wasn't like a mother but like a drill sergeant, barking orders. Mum said that, "life had made Granny hard so that she couldn't or wouldn't bend. So hard, that I couldn't wait to get away from her, to leave school to marry, anyone. Just so that I could get away." It was hard to hear the critical voice of my Mum as she described an earlier version of my grandmother. But it was her truth, so she just said it as she saw it. No poison or malice, just stating the facts. She also said that Granny had changed so much since we were born. She couldn't believe how much grandchildren had softened her, made her into the mother that my Mum wished that she'd had.

I can't imagine that 'hard' woman that my Mum described, but I can imagine that life was hard for Granny. She never talked about it, but it was there, I could feel it when I hugged her – the sorrow, the aloneness that was deep inside her. She would hold me tight when we hugged sometimes and she would sigh quietly, and exhale, "oh child . . ." holding me tighter, for a moment longer than she should have. And there it was. Pain all wrapped up in a cuddle. But it never came out often. She lived more in the present, hardly talked of her past, and enjoyed the life that she had made.

Her bone china plates sat proudly in a cabinet in one corner of the living room along with her crystal glasses and dainty cups and saucers. The silverware also lived there in a drawer, and this, along with the perfect plates and glasses, was used at dinner time every day. In the bottom of the cabinet, behind closed doors were treats and snacks. We all knew where to go to get monkey nuts, crisps, peanut brittle, or Murray Mints and the cupboard was always well stocked every time we visited. A gleaming redwood dining table sat off to one side, and her sofa and armchair completed the furniture in the snug living room. There was a lot going on, which could have looked cluttered but, she had her own style and an eye for detail, which meant that she could do so much with very little money and space. In another corner sat the TV that she hardly watched as she was a radio person. She listened to 'The Archers' religiously and kept up to date with the news, politics and current events through talk shows on BBC Radio Four. She had come a long way since the fifties and she was proud, grateful for everything that she owned – polishing, cleaning and displaying it all with pride. It hadn't always been like that though.

Back when we were much smaller, Granny used to live in two rooms, at the top of a ten-room house in Lordship Lane – surrounded by the orthodox Jewish community. When we stayed over, she always let us listen to story time on the radio before we went to bed. We used to all fit in her bed on our sleepovers – don't ask me how – while she'd sleep in the other room, on the floor. She had a crucifix on the bedroom wall which looked harmless during the day, a little thing that took pride of place in the centre, facing the bed. We'd settle down to go to sleep and after kisses goodnight, Granny would shut the door and welcome in the pitch black. The curtains at the large window were lined to keep the cold out, let in not a whisper of air, nor a slither of light. Complete blackness settled in the room, and then, the terror came.

On the wall, gazing down on us was Jesus Christ himself, floating in the air. He seemed to sway and hover above our heads, moving from side to side, looking sorrowful and dejected. It literally seemed as though the body of Christ was coming towards me, which was too much for me to bear. I'd shut my eyes tight to blot out the glowing presence and try not to let the fright overcome me. After saying 'The Lord's Prayer, followed by a bunch of 'Hail Marys', I think I probably passed out with fear. We all hated that bloody thing. That, and the mice that could climb curtains, was my enduring memory from that time.

As we got older, we still visited, but I tended to be on my own as my siblings didn't really see the point of it. Granny had moved on to live in a warden-assisted flat in Stoke Newington and I loved going to visit her and being in the familiar smell and vibe that was her home. It was peaceful and elegant, just as she was.

As I watched the endless re-runs of the old black and white movies on Sundays, I thought of Granny. The women in these movies had a classiness and beauty that I could relate to, that I recognised. Immaculately dressed, as they lived in their beautiful world. Bette Davis, Judy Garland and Joan Crawford were my favourite actresses while Sidney Poitier and Harry Belafonte were my secret crush. They had this inner strength, an integrity, as well as another side – a 'don't mess with me' side. Complicated people that made everything appear like life was easy, effortless. Of course, nothing was in those days, but they made it seem like it was so, all of which reminded me of my Granny. She'd lived to see so much, the hardship of being a fisherman's daughter, then moving from Trinidad to England on her own. But she never lost her spirit. She was a strong and sometimes scarily intense black woman, but to me she was just Granny.

She decided to come to Britain from Trinidad during the fifties, as part of the 'Wind Rush' generation. As one of eight siblings on the move during this time, she was the only one that came to England with no contacts, no family, and not a lot of money. The professional work that was promised to immigrants never materialised, and she started piece-work machining, as a means of earning a living. It wasn't what she expected, but she never complained. Why she was the only one in the family to come to England was a mystery. She never talked about it. But, she always kept in contact with the family as it scattered across the world.

She was a private person who kept to herself, who had a great well of feeling although she showed little emotion. She would laugh and was fun to be around, but there was a separateness that she maintained, and she wasn't a person that you would mess with. She was focused and scraped and went without for years, so that she could save for my mother's passage to England. My Mum finally arrived when she was fourteen. If we could get Granny in the mood to talk, she would describe how it was in the early days. "I would have black tea for breakfast and lunch, and potatoes with onion for dinner. Once a week I would buy bacon, no other meat, and flour and more potatoes to make flat bread. Huh . . . lived on that for yearsssss, and never cook potato now. Ever." Granny was the type of woman who would grit her teeth and get on with whatever life threw her way. My mum wasn't like that though. She hated coming to this cold country, with cold people, she was forever saying, every winter.

". . . lonely an alone an hated Mammy for bringing mi to this god-forsaken country, leaving all my cousins and friends behind," my Mum told me once. "Never really got over it an hated her too." She said it in that laughing way that adults do, when they try to make out their joking – and you know that they really mean it. I sensed that there was something between my Mum and Granny, but didn't get it. They never argued or anything, but something was just a little off, I could feel it. But thIngs changed when my Dad left to go to America. And I noticed that around that time, Mum and Granny became a lot closer too.

Granny was calm, and never raised her voice, not at us or at anyone. Instead, when she'd had enough of us yelling and fighting, she would break into French patois and say a few choice words. We didn't speak French, but we definitely spoke 'Granny' and understood what was behind her words. We knew she wasn't happy when she started speaking patois and never considered what would happen if we didn't do as we were told. We always listened to Granny, in fact, everyone listened when she spoke. She had that kind of headmistress vibe. She was a permanent feature while my Mum worked hard to bring us up on her own, and as a result, she was as familiar to me as my Mum. Sometimes, maybe more so, as I could tell that I was a lot like her.

We played scrabble, she showed me how to cook, to sew by hand, embroidery and crocheting. Eventually I was allowed on the magical sewing machine. I felt very grown up and together as I sat on her sewing chair raised with cushions and sewed wonky seams and played around with scraps of material. After a while, I did improve, but was never great, which didn't matter to her though. She always looked at the stuff I worked on like it was the most wonderful creation, and that made me feel like I was amazing, an artist, talented even. I was relaxed and at home with her, she was familiar in smell, in sight, and sound, and had the softest skin to touch. No wrinkles, no splotches, or spots – ever.

It was probably because of all those things that I ended up at Granny's flat in a subdued mood after my doctor's visit, as I had a lot on my mind. I was never an 'in your face' kind of kid, but I was talkative because I was inquisitive. I asked the most amount of questions about all number of things and she would take the time to answer every one thoroughly and unhurriedly. If she didn't know the answer she wouldn't try and fob you off, or tell you a bunch of nonsense like some adults did to look smart. She would say, "hmmmm, you know I don't know," and we'd investigate. For me to have someone who would have the patience to listen and teach like that was something that I looked forward to. This was not the case at home. My Mum had five kids and she didn't like me asking questions. Maybe it was because she didn't have the time or the energy to answer back – who knows! I couldn't put my finger on why, but I remember that when I got to a certain age, I stopped asking her questions as I could sense that it irritated her. She always recounted stories of her children to friends and she would have me tagged as the talker. But I felt no pride when she said it. It felt negative, even to my childish ears. So, I learnt to stop asking questions and talking too much – except with Granny.

But not today. She must have known that something was up as she kept plying me with food and sarsaparilla. We both listened to a talk show on the radio and I sorted some wool from the crochet basket on my lap, while she cooked coo coo, ochre, spinach, green banana and red mullet. Eventually, she came into the living room and, wiped her hands on a hand-towel. She then sat in her favourite armchair and shuffled around a bit, and when she was comfortable, she asked me what was going on. I didn't answer at first and pretended that I was engrossed in her thimble collection that was displayed on the wall. She waited, and I continued to look at the wall for awhile. Then without thinking, I blurted out what had happened with Dr Patel as hot tears rolled down my cheeks. I wiped my tears and snot on the back of my arm and was surprised when more started coming, faster.

When I'd finished, she just sat with her hands folded in her lap, tea towel wrapped around her fingers, saying nothing, doing nothing, just sitting. She was actually so still that I peeked a look up through my sniffles and saw that she was, well, sad. She just stared off in the distance and sat there rigidly, and silent. This was scary and uncharted territory for me. I'd never seen my Granny upset before and couldn't believe that she was capable of something so ordinary as sadness. She was invincible, a superwoman, my hero. The fact that I had made her unhappy was too much, and made me feel even worse than before. I started to cry even louder now thinking that I'd done something wrong by making such a fuss and causing her distress. Unlike me, her sadness and silence didn't spill out into a wet mess and didn't last very long. But I could tell that she was crying on the inside. Eventually I stopped and we sat there, together in silence. She sighed heavily and told me to gather my thoughts. Then she said, "when I sweep the floor, I would sweep it out the house, take all the dirt I can see and throw it in the dustbin." I listened carefully as I knew that something profound was about to happen, that I was going to learn a magical truth. She continued, "I pay special attention to the corners because things can stay lost or stay hidden. Then it would be taken away by the dustman and would no longer be part of life."

"Oookay..." I thought, not really following, "I'm sure this will all become clear." I listened more carefully, wondering if I might have missed something. "Then the sunshine would come out and shine directly through the window on the floor, and more dirt would be revealed. That is when the real opportunity to clean would appear."

"Okay you've got me," I thought. I'd no idea what she was talking about. In fact, she wasn't even looking at me to see if I'd made sense of it. She almost seemed to be talking to herself. I could tell that this was not the time to show my ignorance, to ask awkward questions, or breathe too heavily. So, I kept my mouth shut, and waited. And waited some more.

She went into the kitchen, turned off the fire under the cooking pots, pulled out a dining table chair and faced me. She leaned into me and said, "it was not your fault, you understand." I stared at her and in my mind, I took on-board what she was saying, but I just couldn't understand why she was still angry. My face must have indicated confusion because she then said, "this doctor mistreated you, your sister and your friend yes?" I didn't want to say the wrong thing, but I thought it would be okay to nod, so I did. "So, he will have done the same to many girls of your age, if not younger," she finished. As I listened closely, I began to see where she was going with it, understanding what she was suggesting in a way that I'd never considered before. I liked her reasoning, but made sure to keep my mouth shut, which was a good thing as I made another quantum connection. I realised that she was not angry with me – her anger was with him!

While she talked, I blew my nose and breathed a sigh of relief, firstly because she believed me, and secondly because I knew that I'd done the right thing in telling her all about it. She asked me loads of questions about him, about the surgery, more about him, where it was, who worked with him, and by the end of her firing question after question at me, she stopped and held out her arms for a hug. I sank into her, into her familiar and safe caress, and she said, "hugs are the best thing in the world, you know," and of course she was right. It felt so good. We stayed together for awhile, then pulled apart and smiled at each other in an amicable silence. She got up and put the fire back on under the pots, and we continued with the rest of the afternoon as though nothing out of the ordinary had happened. It was never mentioned again.

That night as I lay in bed going over what had occurred, I remembered that my mood was lighter and that on my walk home I no longer had that feeling of dread, doom, despair or whatever it was in my tummy. The heaviness was gone. I was finally able to make peace with what had happened with Dr Patel. As Granny would say when things puzzled her, "it didn't sit right on my chest, you know." Telling Granny was like being purged of the badness. I knew that I would never be able to forget all that came from that horrible day but now, I also knew that I was in no way to blame for what he did.

***

A few months later my Mum took my younger sister to the doctor and came back with a new set of medications for her coughing and cold. She'd had a bad chest again and Dr Patel always prescribed the same medication, much to my Mum's disgust, as they never worked. She kept on telling him, but he just pumped out the same prescriptions, "as if he had shares in the drug company," she would say. On this occasion however, things were different. I heard her telling our neighbour that she had seen a new doctor, and that she was really impressed with the way that she'd listened before scribbling out the prescription. Now this particular neighbour, Pearlie, had a way of getting gossip so quickly, that it was frightening. She always knew who did what to who, when, why and how, quicker than was comfortably possible. If our estate was a quiet country village, then she was the village gossip. Unfortunately, she took pride in her ability to talk about literally everyone, and she didn't care whether it was appropriate, hurtful or truthful information that she was peddling. Today was no different as she had news that was hot off the press. She was delighted in being able to be the bearer of glad tidings, as they stood outside their front doors.

"So, it seems like Dr Patel wa sacked and im hav im licence tek way," was how she opened her story. I was a fully functioning nosy twelve-year-old, who didn't really listen to grown up stuff, but even I knew a good story was on its way. So, I moved in closer to the front door where the grownups were talking, so I could ear wig on their conversation. My Mum must've indicated that she was obviously suspicious of this news, so our neighbour gave the credentials of her source, to show that she knew what she was talking about. "Yuh know how Margie is mi good fren?, yuh know who me a taak bout – the receptionist? Margie eena di surgery," she continued, pausing for dramatic effect. "Well, (she rolled her eyes - and boy, did she have big eyes) it seem dat Dr Patel a now Mr Patel bikaaz im was a naughty boy."

"Uh huh" my Mum encouraged. Then she broke into full patois, which she did sometimes. She'd flip back and forth from sounding like a proper white woman, back to her black roots in a heartbeat. They all did it. "Mi never kno that yuh and she wa fren," she added suspiciously.

"Yeah man, we travel way bac," said Pearlie. I managed to peek at them as they talked and noticed that Pearlie seemed a little put out at the interruption. She looked at my Mum as if to say, "do you want me to keep talking?" With her eyebrow raised, arms folded. My Mum guessed that she was at the point of clamming up, so she didn't say another word. The awkward silence must have been enough for Pearlie to feel that she could continue with her story. "Oh yes, dem tek way im license bikaaz ima kiddie fiddler," our neighbour said in a conspiratorial stage whisper.

"SAY WHA? HOW YUH MEAN?" Mum said loudly, obviously in shock. The way that she had yelled out the sentence meant that she had been caught off guard and was totally hooked!

"Shhhh, yuh waan the whole world fi know? Yeah man, im a perve. She say dem did ketch im at fi im previous surgery, but since dem couldn't prove anything, dem let im off. Den im come here fi practice."

By this time, I had moved even closer to the conversation and Sandra had come out of the living room and was listening too. Another neighbour from the floor above had just come up the stairs with her shopping and had caught the last bit of the gossip. She greeted the two women and putting down her bags on the landing, joined the conversation. Now that our story telling neighbour had an audience, she played to the crowd and became quite animated.

"So," Pearlie continued looking at them both to make sure that they were paying attention, "im couldn't keep im dutty hands to himself and im start to touch up di gyal dem down this side."

"How yuh mean?" asked my Mum more quietly. All the fun had gone from her voice and I could tell that she was no longer entertained but concerned. She'd had a chance to process Pearlie's information and seemed a bit on edge.

"Ah wa yuh a seh?" exclaimed the neighbour with the shopping called Maisie.

"Yuh kno, dem tittie an ting "Pearlie went on. By this time I was squirming on the inside. I looked over at my sister and could tell that she was feeling the same way too. Pearlie continued, "this time, im get ketch by some next doctor, from some fancy hospital in the City. One of fi im nurse pickney di get abuse and dem report im, nasty bloodclaat," Pearlie finished, shaking her head in disgust. By this time, I'd started to recall my conversation with Granny. I remembered the questions, after questions, and began to wonder . . . I then dismissed my thoughts.

"How many girls im did mess wid?" my Mum asked.

"Boy, who kno," said Pearlie. Suddenly, her demeanour changed, and she became less animated. She realised that her audience seemed worried, and eventually she put her hand to her mouth in shock. "Gyal, all I know is dat some a di mothers di complain about im, but it never come to much." There was a pause, and quietly Pearlie asked "yuh did ever complain?" She looked at my Mum and Maisie who both shook their heads negatively. Sandra and I looked at each other from our hiding place near the door and I looked away quickly, uncomfortable with the glassy eyed stare that she gave me. I had no idea what she was thinking – and didn't want to know.

"Always da same, always da same. Nobody ever believe we. Have to be one of fi im own people to mek a bad ting betta," said Maisie from upstairs knowingly. "Cha" was her parting word as she picked up her shopping and carried on climbing the stairs to her flat. My mum closed the door suddenly and looked at my sister and me. She became aware that we were listening to the conversation and we jumped out of our skins at the suddenness of being caught eavesdropping. We froze and she held our stare silently. We looked at her with trepidation.

"Yuh hear wha was said?" she asked. We couldn't quite work out if we were in trouble for listening to 'big people tings'. My sister and I looked at each other and telepathically decided that honesty was the best policy. "Huh," was all my Mum said after we answered, before walking off into the kitchen to cook.

I may have forgotten to mention that Granny had moved away from machining years ago and was a theatre nurse in one of the specialist hospitals in Central London. So, maybe the criss-cross questioning that she'd put me through was more important than I'd realised. As I went into my room to think about what I'd just heard, I flopped down on my bed to consider a thought.

Could it be . . .?

. . .What are the odds?

I swirled around Pearlie's story in my mind, and finally concluded that my Granny must have had something to do with Dr Patel getting the boot. I just knew it! It was too much of a coincidence.

I never mentioned my conversation with Granny to anyone nor did I talk with her about it ever again. But I constantly tried to make sense of what she said about sweeping away the dirt. I didn't find the courage to ask her what she actually meant, because well, she probably wouldn't have told me. We were close, but not that close. There was an invisible line that couldn't be crossed when talking to your elders while they shared information, and I'd learnt when not to ask questions. She'd once said to me when I asked her to clarify a conversation that we had awhile back, "if you didn't understand then child, how you expect to understand now? Words take on all sorts of meanings, when let out in the air to breathe." What the heck did that mean? She always did that, truths and riddles mixed into one. I was none the wiser from her answer and wished I'd never asked.

Either way, I was glad that I didn't have to see that man again and I know I wasn't the only child that felt that way.

Fourteen

I'd pretty much avoided alcohol during my teenage years as it seemed to bring out some of the strangest things in people. My biggest influence had to be my Mum who would unfortunately turn into a pit bull terrier after a few drinks. Normally she was a sweet, friendly lady who had a light personality and was really fun. She loved to play-fight with us when we were small, rolling us all around the room with her soft, cuddly, roly-poly body squishing the air from our lungs. We'd only give in after she squashed us into submission. She also liked to play other games. Her favourites were dominoes and cards and as we got older, we played most Sundays during the cold winter evenings. I loved playing with my Mum, because she took it seriously, and, she was good. She'd seat herself at the table with a fag dangling from between her fingers as she flicked and clicked her other nails between each play. I'd copy her, taking my time between moves, studying the cards and pretending that I had a plan. Meanwhile she'd chew on her bottom lip and take her time to slaughter us. I loved playing games with her as it was a kind of respite for us, from the other stuff in our everyday lives.

To say that things were difficult and that we were up against it was an understatement. But, we were fortunate in that when I was around twelve, we moved. I'm not sure what made our move to such a posh location possible, but it was long overdue. The estate had become progressively dirty and unkempt and many of our original friends had moved elsewhere. Over time, the whole estate closed down for repairs as one by one, families were moved elsewhere. I was sad to go, but I had outgrown the playground and the library and had moved on to secondary school. Because I craved new experiences, I started piano and violin lessons and began to sketch and draw in my spare time. I lost myself in the hugeness of Hackney Central Library, and as I'd been given an adult registration card early, I was able to access all the books that the library had to offer.

We eventually moved to a four-bedroom semi-detached house in South Hackney. This was hands down like hitting the jackpot because it was in the prettiest part of town. Our house had just been decorated and was ready to move into and, it was unlike anything that we'd ever lived in before. It was a massive house, split into two flats, and we had the top part which straddled three floors.

It was light and airy, spacious, and sat in a short cul-de-sac, that led directly into a common parkland at the far end of the road. This became our local stomping ground, and it was glorious. The amount of space that we had was unreal, to scream at the top of our voices, mucking around until we'd literally run out of breath, and then mucking around some more. In the summer we'd climb trees and lay in the lush grass on our backs, making plans and making shapes out of the clouds. In the winter, if it snowed, we'd be out at the crack of dawn making shapes on the untouched snow in what we called 'The Common'. Up until that point, I'd lived my life in a concrete jungle, and suddenly, I was exposed to space and nature like I'd never seen before. Victoria Park, a huge, expansive grassland, with a bowling green, a nature reserve, a massive play park, and more flowers than was necessary, was just beyond the Common.

The Common and Victoria Park extended into each other, separated only by a road with a zebra crossing. All day every day was spent outdoors while Sandra, me, and a few others, explored what the area had to offer. The Common was a circle which also edged into many council housing blocks which were all clustered in one area, plonked together it seemed, so as not to spill out into the posher areas nearby. These blocks reminded me of where I used to live, and I avoided them like the plague. The flats all opened into a concrete courtyard, but unlike my old estate, there was no real space to play or to breathe. Living in those flats would be like being trapped in a prison I imagined, and I wanted nothing to do with it. Some of our friends, on the other hand, lived in these estates, and saw nothing wrong with living on the seventeenth floor of a high-rise block. To be honest, there was nothing wrong with where they lived but, my thinking had shifted, and I'd begun to see myself differently. Suddenly, I lived in a posh house and went to a grammar school and didn't see myself as that kid that lived in a council estate anymore. I wasn't clear about what I'd become, but I was sure that I was no longer a regular kid anymore. Until it was time to hang out and all of those differences were forgotten.

The Common was common land to us all, as posh or poor, we all backed into its circular shape and could walk right in, as it was without special entrances, exits or barriers. Some of our friends lived in houses – in our street, or other streets that backed directly into the Common – while others lived on the estate around its edges. It didn't matter. We all found ourselves and each other as we all played together regardless.

I suddenly felt that I could breathe, without realising that I'd been holding my breath. I also found myself noticing the sky – with its many shades of blue and ever-changing clouds – which I hadn't known that I'd been missing. I felt alive and more comfortable in my skin in my new home, and it was a nice feeling. I sighed with relief when we moved, and I knew it would be good for us. We needed good.

I can remember some of the signs that all was not well from my Mum's point of view though. For instance, we had carpet fitted throughout the four flights of stairs in the house, a multicoloured Axminster, which was a really good quality. The living room was carpeted at the same time and linoleum was laid in the kitchen, bathroom and toilet. There was also bedding for four bedrooms, towels and curtains for all rooms and for the massive window in the hallway. A new sofa was installed, a brown hairy thing that swallowed everyone that sat in it and, because it was made of some kind of shaggy cloth, kept me warm on chilly nights. These things just appeared. As if from nothing, came something. But it's never quite as simple as that. Because, as a single parent on social security, money was a real problem for my Mum. We lived on a shoestring basically and, there was no spare cash in our house. Ever. I reckon it must have worried the hell out of her, but luckily, she was able to cope. How?

We had a regular Saturday visitor that was called the 'Provident Man'. This was how we coped. He didn't even have a name, though he came to our house regular as clockwork every week, for years. He was just known as the 'Provident Man'. He was introduced to my Mum through a friend, an average, pale-looking english guy, with intense eyes and a permanent smile. I could tell she didn't like him as she always pulled her arms around herself, as if she was cold when she answered his knock on the door. But that wasn't what mattered, as our lives changed drastically after that. Gone was the tightness round her mouth, the snapping, short temper and the strained look on her face when we ran out of food, or fuel or both. In came the goods, and the smell of new, new, new. Everything that was needed was purchased on credit for stupid prices with tons of interest piled on top. My Mum was sucked into more and more debt as she bought the stuff we needed and the stuff she wanted, on credit. It was like Christmas had come early when we saw all this new stuff arriving, piece by piece. My mum looked relieved and started playing with us again. It was always a good sign when she played, one of the signs I noticed, that indicated that she wasn't worried. Other times, it would show in how much she smoked. The more she smoked, the higher the stress. And sometimes it would show in how much she drank, but not often. Things had taken a turn for the better and at first, every weekend when he knocked, my mum would fetch her purse and go down and meet him. She had a little book that he gave her, but she barely looked at it. She just chucked it on the top of the fridge carelessly, along with all the other unopened letters, until Saturday came around.

Eventually, my Mum became restless and resentful of the whole 'payback what you owe contract' that exists when you buy stuff on the drip. It happened while we lived on the estate, and it was happening again, but at a posher address. She just didn't have the patience for debts, and she wouldn't deal with it well. It wasn't as if she didn't understand finance, as she worked as a bookkeeper for awhile. But, as she once said after she'd had a few drinks inside her, "It's too much yuh know? every week, after week – too hard." I genuinely think that she just got bored. And eventually, she would decide that she needed something else, something new, and she'd pick up another provident man and rack up more debt. It was the circle of life for us – and it was how our family survived. I was aware of the situation growing up as a child; the lack of money, the tension and the fear that something bad would happen because we never had enough. It wasn't 'in your face' obvious, but it was registering with me in a subtle way. I could feel it creeping around in the shadows, not really thinking about it, or conscious of it, just observing and absorbing it all.

So many times, we turned off the telly and pretended that we weren't in when they came knocking. Sometimes they would just keep on knocking and in the end, my Mum would send one of us down to the front door to say that she wasn't in. I hated that. I hated the feeling that I felt when we didn't have the money to pay him. It made me feel like I'd done something wrong, like it was my fault, like I was a bad person. I remember thinking that I would never get credit as a grown up, as I didn't want to feel that feeling – of not being able to afford to pay it back. The pressure of these men banging on our front door, and then having to hide in the hope that they would go away, was not an experience that I wanted to take into my adulthood.

My mum didn't have the luxury of feeling anything, other than the need to survive, as she found yet another provident man, and we'd get a brand-new cooker or fridge. He came on

Thursday, so we were never in on that day either. She also took credit from the milk man, who delivered milk at four o'clock in the morning. We'd never had that before, as they didn't do deliveries in the estates. That's probably because they couldn't leave their floats unattended, as their bits and bobs would get nicked as soon as they turned their backs. It was brilliant that he came to the house as the nearest shop was quite a bit away, and we couldn't just 'pop to the shops' when things ran out. He made a fortune as he also sold bread, eggs, bacon, and sausages. He was like a mini grocery store on wheels, turning up on the doorstep offering tea, sugar and anything else that you might forget to buy during the weekly shop, So, she ran up a massive bill and we ended up avoiding him as well when he came for collection, early Friday morning. It felt ridiculous telling him that my Mum wasn't in when he came for payment at the crack of dawn. I didn't like having to lie to any of them, and in the end, she used to send me to the front door, and I used to send my younger siblings so I wouldn't have to confront any of it. "What kind of useless Mum is she," I would think every time she missed a payment. But, I remember that my disgust eventually turned into respect as I became older. Like she said, "I hav fi do wha I hav fi do, as mi hav five kids to look after on my own, and nobody printing money on behalf fi mi." She made it work. She had to juggle, she had to hustle, and she made it work.

There weren't any next-door neighbours that she could borrow from when she fell short. It wasn't that kind of neighbourhood. We lived in a place where people kept to themselves and didn't really mingle and mix. Our street was wide, lined with trees, without clutter and broken paving stones. Instead, it had families where the men went out to work in a suit and tie, and came back in the evening at dinner time, looking tired, and glad to come home. Families with children called 'Sam' or 'Naomi' and even 'Hugo' or 'Pippa', smallish families with two or three children. Families with animals such as cats, dogs, fish, rabbits, guinea pigs and gerbils. It had everything and anything on our road – except black people.

We were the first black family to live on our road, which meant nothing to me at the time, but could have meant everything to my Mum. We weren't a talkative family, so never had a conversation about why we moved or what was going on in my Mums' grown-up world and her adult mind. That was never considered the business of the child. And so, I never really understood the social changes that happened when we moved into that neighbourhood. But it was there. It didn't create any obvious differences for me, but for my Mum, it must have taken some getting used to. The invisibility of everything and everyone was definitely not how we did things. Quiet, sedate, calm (I had to look those words up, as it wasn't a part of my vocabulary) was how I would describe it. In an estate, there is no real privacy, and everyone could hear everything, even when the front door banged shut and the curtains swished closed. The walls were thin, and people were loud, unless they had something to hide. Estate life was noisy and full of hidden energy, and there was always something going on. Living in our new street, in our huge house wasn't like that. I'm not sure that my Mum liked her new environment, I'm not sure if my Mum felt comfortable until eventually, another black family moved in. Bernadette was a woman on her own, with two sons and her sister. My mum literally breathed a sigh of relief and immediately became firm friends with our new neighbour. At last, she had someone to borrow sugar from.

**

Fast forward to age fourteen, and nothing much had changed. The carpet in the hallway was the same, but now it was worn through to the point where the wood could be seen, and we could be heard clumping and clunking as we ran up and down the stairs. The bedding had long since lost its lustre and been replaced and the sofa was broken on one side. We still dodged the weekly salesmen, but the milkman had disappeared, along with the paraffin man and the coal man, who all went out of business. We ended up having to walk to get milk virtually every day and gas, electric and Calor gas heating replaced the coal fire and paraffin heater. I remember that I never felt warm in our house in the beginning. It was as if it couldn't hold on to heat with its high ceilings, big windows, and tons of stairs. Compared to where we used to live, it felt cold in the spring and summer, and freezing for the rest of the year.

Eventually, I got used to the coldness of our house, street, and neighbours. It took awhile, but we were able to inject our warmth and vibrancy into the house and make it our home. It took a bit longer to conquer the street, as our neighbours had obviously never lived around people like us before. We were noisy, we were untidy, and we were the only house on the street that didn't give a hoot about the state of our garden. We were friendly and outgoing and eventually our neighbours loosened up, a little. We rubbed along, becoming firm friends with Bernadette and her family, while being 'warm, but distant' with the rest of the families on the street. My Mum worked nights as a nurse now that we were older, and although we were marginally better off, she kept things simple, making things work like she always did.

Because Sandra went to a mixed comprehensive school, she knew quite a few boys. They loved coming round to our house and hanging with . . . my Mum. She was great fun, loved the same type of music as we did and was easy to be around. Sometimes we'd have as much as a dozen guys chilling at our house, some playing cards, others telling stories and the rest playing dominoes. I couldn't work out why they liked to come to our house all the time, but my Mum was very smart and knew exactly what she was doing. She used to say to her friends, "listen, mi hav two teenage girls and need to mak sure mi can keep an eye on them, yuh know? Mi haffi know who them hanging with, and whether them is decent guys mi can trust."

"I hear yuh," her friends would say, but I could tell that they thought that my Mum was a bit 'out there'. None of them let their kids have the freedom that we had. Nor did they trust their kids the way my Mum trusted us – and the guys. In return, she offered fun and games, a relaxed atmosphere and a warm place to hang during the cold winter months. She once explained to me that it was better that they came to the house rather than, "yuh lot sneaking round street corners making di neighbourhood look untidy," as she put it. She was the only parent that I knew that thought like that, and I really think that she was ahead of her time in this aspect. I also think that she was an even better mum because of it.

I once spoke with her, trying to find out the reason why she wasn't a typical mum. She wasn't one for talking about herself, but one day I caught her off guard.

"When mi cum to dis country mi was a kid, a little younger than yuh. I didn't want fi come and mi didn't want fi live with your Granny. No suh." She saw my shocked look and held up her hands in a defensive stance. "Hol on, hol on, it's not what yuh think." To be honest, I couldn't understand why she would say that about her own Mum, my Granny. It was the first criticism of Granny that I had ever heard, and I wasn't sure if I liked it. "You have fi look at it from my side," she continued. "I was at home in Trinidad, living wid my Granny an staying wid my aunties, while your Granny was in England, trying to hustle up di money fi mi fare. I was wid my cousins, mi was like fi dem sister, and we used to do everything together. That was my home." I could tell that she was getting lost in the memories from her voice. It was the sound of someone who is remembering something good, which brings a smile to the lips and a warmth to the tone.

"But Mum," I said. "How could you say that! I would want to be with you always," I finished self-consciously.

"Wha would I wan fi cum here fah? I had nobody!" She said harshly. The smile was gone and was replaced by bitterness. "It was cold, cold cold like mi never kno it could be, and the people dem was horrible. I had no one – no cousins, no aunties an my Granny was gone. It was just me. And your Granny. And she wasn't like she is now," she scowled. I could tell that it wasn't a happy memory anymore. I was surprised that she was even talking about it, because she normally kept her feelings to herself.

"What do you mean? What was she like?" I asked, knowing that I might not like the answer.

"She was horrible," she said flatly. "She was hard, hard as nails, and she never ha a smile or a good word fi me. She would work fi long hours and I was always on my own, in this cold arse country. Huh!" She paused, and I thought that's it. I mean, I thought that I'd hit the mother load. She had NEVER talked like this before. That's not who we were. We weren't the kind of people who shared our emotions and talked things through – ever. That stuff only happened on the telly or in books.

I was fascinated by that side of my Mum, because she kept it hidden, and only let us see her, really see her, once in a while. So, instead of feeling like I had to defend Granny from my Mums bad-mouthing, I decided to pay attention and really listen as my Mum continued. "Then she put me eena dat school with horrible people – no black children. Well . . ." And then she stopped. She thought for awhile. "There was one black girl, but she didn't count bikaaz she might as well hav been white." She sniffed when she said that, to show her distain. "Look, all I'm saying is dat she wasn't like she is now, and I couldn't wait fi get weh from her"

"Oh, I didn't realise . . ." I started to say, but she cut me off.

"Nobody realise! Who was I going to tell? When I did get pregnant with your sister mi couldn't wait fi leave and get married."

"But why? What was so bad?" I didn't get it. I knew that she would clam up soon, and I really wanted to understand this little piece of her life.

"I was lonely." She said sadly. "It wa so cold in this here country. Do you kno dat the first-time mi see snow, lord, it was so beautiful. Mi cum home from school and mi ha fi pee, and I was waiting fi Mammy fi cum home from work. So, I stooped down out in the back, pee'd in the snow, and get an infection in mi womb. It hurt so bad and put mi in bed fi weeks. And . . . cha, I would lay in bed in a hitch up room, in a brock down house in the freezing cold and wonder what the hell mi was doing here. I wasn't used to it – being alone. I always had my cousins, my Granny. They was my family and here, there was nothing. Just Mammy. I couldn't get to meet anyone as she wouldn't let mi go anywhere or do anything bikaaz she didn't truss. But then, why would she truss anybody? Everybody was on a hustle and dem white people wa rude and nasty to us dem times. Dem not so bad now, but dem times? Lord have mercy." She gave a little laugh and shook her head slowly. "Mi didn't choose fi cum here. Huh, Mi didn't want fi cum here at all." She shuddered, and it seem to wake her out of that time. "Gyal, it was hard," she finished. Memory over. Dead.

Our friends in contrast, had more traditional black parents who came to England as adults, from choice. Parents that were like my Mums description of how my Granny used to be. Focussed, unsmiling people, that were suspicious of all friendships that their girl children had, and were especially hostile to all boys. Because of this, it was normal for our friends not to mention to their parents that they had any kind of friendships at all, as often they would go crazy and ban it immediately. Our friends also found it difficult to get permission to go anywhere, and quite a few of them sneaked out of their houses to go to the youth club or to parties. It was definitely one rule for girls and one for boys. Girls were chained to the house with chores and routine, while boys got to run free. It was common for them to risk a beating, just to get a little air, a little freedom. Sneaking out, just to be able to socialise. Some of them got away with it, but most of them didn't. I kinda sensed that it was their parents' way of trying to protect their daughters from getting pregnant – before their time. Before they'd had a chance to live a little life and be successful. To make their suffering and hardship in Britain worthwhile. But it didn't work. From what I can remember, my friends that did get pregnant before they were sixteen were the ones that were under lock and key and never allowed out at all.

Thankfully, my Mum had a different attitude which paid dividends. We learnt how to form relationships with boys that went beyond the usual boy/girl equals sex stuff. We built wonderful friendships with boys which lasted us throughout our teenage years. They were funny, great company, and loved to muck around. They were also our personal minders who protected us when we went out to clubs and parties, making sure that we arrived home safely. They were like a gaggle of brothers who were also our mates.

There was a small group of guys who were regular visitors which my Mum liked the most. They all went to the youth club that we attended on Mondays, and she knew most of their mothers. Daniel was the eldest, a songbird who was forever singing and the smoothest dancer ever. I loved going to parties with him as he was the kind of guy that had to keep moving. He was so light on his feet that he seemed to glide everywhere, and he swayed and jived his way around a room with every move that he made. He wasn't the best-looking guy, but he sure was the most lyrical. He had a lightness that I haven't ever seen in a person, like he was connected to a parallel world. If we went to a party or a dance, he'd sing along to practically every record and then it would all get too much for him. He'd then grab me or whoever was next to him to dance, he couldn't help himself. He was a great mover, and I could pick up his steps quickly as we danced together so often. His energy was infectious, and it felt effortless when I danced with him. He was like the big brother I would have liked to have, fun to be around and really only interested in having a great time. With him, it was always guaranteed that that would be the case. His nickname was 'Bird'

Clayton was another constant. He was always the worrier of our group. He would make sure that we got home on time, that we didn't drink or get into trouble. He kept one eye on Sandra, and the other eye on me, so that we weren't exposed to any guys that weren't up to his standards. I called him the big brother that you didn't want to have. Although he was quite short for his age, he was broad and strong, and you wouldn't want to get into a fight with him. In his spare time, he was on his school athletics team, at county level, and he was also pretty good at football. He hung out at New River Athletics Club in Tottenham, which was a famous training ground, and was hoping to get into the national team. He got his nick name 'Hitler' because he was bossy and such a stickler for time and for always making sure that we did the right thing.

Colin was the younger brother of Daniel, who was fun to be with but was never the ringleader. He was the watcher of the group. He'd sit there listening while we all talked and laughed about, not saying much but always present, nevertheless. He would wait and time his input, dropping one liners and gags here and there, effortlessly, and would have us in stitches of laughter. He was more aware of black politics, and always starting conversations about the times that we were living in. He talked about the racial tension that was kicking off in South London way before the Deptford riots took place. It wasn't the sort of thing that we talked about often, but it was there, in the background and didn't need a voice. It was known, ingrained. And wasn't talked about until it was. Just like we didn't talk about the colour of the sky or the leaves on the tree, because they were just, 'there'. He was also the diplomat and managed tensions in the group, stopping some of the banter and bickering that went on, from turning into full on fights.

Trevor, also known as Watson, didn't care about things like that. He was the guy with wandering eyes and hands, had quite a few girls on the go and was the most endearing, loveable guy on the planet. Girls were always fighting over him or fighting to be with him, and he endured it all like a true Casanova. He'd let them scuffle and wrestle it out and the victor got to be his girlfriend, for a day. The fact that girls fought over him made no impression on him at all and he really couldn't get what all the fuss was about. He was a pretty fickle guy to his girlfriends, but he was really lovely to me. We'd talk for hours about music and records and he had an encyclopaedia brain when it came to all things mechanical. He could fix anything. He was killer cute, and had the best-looking afro in east London, which he tended, patted, and shaped up at the barbers practically every week. He even had a little facial hair thing going on, which he managed to rock. He was real close to Hitler and they went everywhere together.

Once, as we all sat around doing nothing in particular, Hitler began to speak. He shot a look at Watson and said, "so, I was at the barbers with Watson and he asked for his usual haircut and . . ."

"No Hitler man," said Watson jumping up from the seat at the table where he'd been playing cards. It was a sudden action – the kind of involuntary movement that you make when your body can't keep up with your mind. "Don't say nothin," he continued in an urgent voice, which was not how he usually spoke at all. Everybody stopped what they were doing and looked from Hitler to Watson. Colin and Bird looked up from watching telly, Sandra paused in painting her nails, Mum quit beating everyone at cards and I stopped reading my book. Watson saw that Hitler had accidentally gotten everybody's attention, and he said again, this time more urgently, "don't say nothin man!"

"Wha ya mean?" said my Mum getting right to the point. "Don't say nothin about wha?" She still held her cards in her hands suspended, as she sensed that Hitler was about to dish some dirt.

"Ah man, Hitler, look what you've gone and done now," said Watson, mortified that all eyes were on him, for all the wrong reasons.

"But I never said anythi . . ." said Hitler, but he didn't get a chance to finish.

"If you don't stop speaking, then I won't set you up with Sonia, you know the one that you reallllly like," said Watson, looking really desperately at Hitler.

"You like Sonia?" asked Sandra. She said it as though she was amazed that anyone would like Sonia. "You do know that she got the clap off Douglas last year, right?" My Mum put her cards down as the game had now been forgotten, while I stared from face to face as I had no idea what was going on.

"Who's Sonia? Did I meet her?" Mum asked.

"NO!" We all said together. Sonia had a bit of a reputation and we'd never hang out with her, let alone bring her home. All the guys knew her well, a bit too well. All the guys it seemed, except Hitler. Hitler looked a bit crushed when he said,

"Watson, why'd you have to bring that up, star. You know that I was only joking."

Joking about wha?" asked Mum. She was plainly getting a bit ratty about being ignored and not being able to keep up with the conversation.

"Whatttttt," said Watson innocently while he looked at Hitler with a 'I told you I'd get you back' look on his face. Hitler paused, had a think, looked at us and said,

"You know that Watson's always in the barbers, so on Saturday we went in and it was packed out, cos it was Mrs Bailey's daughter's wedding. We had to wait ages and when Watson got in the chair, the barber asked how he wanted his cut – you know how they ask you what number blade do ya want, if you want it round or high top, that kinda thing. So, when the barber was finished, he flashed the mirror so Watson could have a look and then . . ." Hitler was interrupted by Watson saying,

"SHUT UP!"

Nobody took any notice of Watson as we were hooked. He sat hunched in his chair and seemed to be the only one who wasn't enjoying the story.

"Wha does this haffi do with Sonia," Mum asked.

"Ssshhhhh," we all said, willing Hitler on to continue.

"Yeah, so the barber took out the mirror and then Watson went and asked for a shape up and everyone in the shop stopped what they were doing, and started laughing and . . ." Hitler had to pause in his story telling as he tried to stifle his laugh. We were all cracking up by this time and I was laughing so hard that my stomach was hurting. Even Hitler had decided to let out his laugh as he retold the story. He continued, "and . . . and then, the barber looked at Watson and said that he'd be happy to give him a shape up and he'd also do his arse for free!" By this time, we'd all fallen around laughing, tears rolling down our cheeks, and even Watson managed a chuckle because it had made us all laugh so hard – all of us, except my Mum.

"So, why yuh all laughing? What's wrong wid his hair! What's so funny," she asked, desperate to get the joke, but couldn't join the dots.

"Mum, they're talking about the three strands of hair on his face that he wanted to shape up," I explained

"Ohhhh, I see," she said, and finally the penny dropped. The fact that Mum still didn't get why it was so funny made us laugh even more, and she was okay with it. We carried on with the evening until the next round of jokes came around.

So, the guys turned up on most nights, after dinner and homework had taken place – sometimes. We'd hang around and laugh and joke and do the stuff that families do to pass the time which could be boring and uneventful, but wasn't. For me, the highlight of my evening was playing cards. We'd all get involved, except Sandra who thought it was a waste of time. As the card playing took off, mini tournaments started to happen. Rummy, Black-jack, Twenty-one and Seven Hundred were some of the games that we'd play, knocking each other out of the tournament until only two players were left. It was intense, exciting and a fun way to pass the time.

Christmas was the best time ever. We'd still do the tree thing, and we still hung tacky paper decorations up in the living room but, it didn't hold the same importance as spending time with the guys meant so much more. My Mum loved to entertain and would start to stash the Christmas booze away at the beginning of December. She had lots of friends, and many club memberships including Freemasons, bingo and dominoes. Christmas was the key time for socialising so, every week Mum would add to her stash. Brandy (her tipple), whisky and vodka and rum would start to appear, along with the usual chasers such as coke, lemonade and ginger beer. Babycham and Cherry B also made an appearance along with Skol lager and a little Blue Nun wine. She asked me to find a space in my wardrobe for some of the stuff, as there was no room in her usual hideaway.

Most nights, my Mum stayed in with us, but sometimes she'd go out. She still allowed the boys to come around though, as she had complete trust in them. On this occasion it was her dominoes night, so off she went leaving my sister in charge with a list of instructions, such as keep the noise down and boys to leave at ten o'clock.

As usual, when the guys arrived, someone started playing records while we eased into playing cards. We started with rummy because it was one of the easier games and each set was likely to be short. In the background, I could hear my sister talking. She didn't really play cards well and was always knocked out early. She decided to mention that my mum had started to buy her collection of Christmas drinks. All ears pricked up and took an interest in what she was saying until she finished off with, "I don't know where Mum has hidden her usual stash." Without thinking, I made my first, fatal mistake. I carried on trashing Hitler at Rummy and, after knocking him out of the tournament, I said triumphantly,

"I know where the stash is." Time stood still as all eyes turned to me. "Oops," I thought then, as I knew that I should have kept my big mouth shut.

"I mean that I know where some of the stash is. . ." I finished more quietly, trickling the last words out. It was too late. I already had everyone's attention. "I mean . . ." My voice petered away into silence. There was a pause.

"Where?" demanded my sister. I could tell that she was annoyed. Probably because I knew something that she didn't.

"I . . . my wardrobe," I muttered vaguely. Before I could get the words out properly, she was rushing upstairs to my room.

"Oh, my gad guys," she hollered, "come help me, there's loads!" She didn't need to say that twice before everyone stopped what they were doing and rushed upstairs.

I remember absently thinking at the time, "Thank God that my bedroom is tidy," as that was the first time that the guys had been upstairs. They came down with Cherry B, Babycham, and some of the lager. Obviously, no-one wanted to play cards any longer, so, looking at my sister for guidance, they waited. Without hesitation, permission was granted, and as she opened a Babycham, the party began. Everybody helped themselves to a beer, except for Hitler and me.

"I really don't think this is a good idea," he began, but by this time, I was the only person listening.

"She'll go crazy," I thought to myself. "Mum's gonna hit the roof." Somebody handed me an open Babycham and without thinking, I put the cute little green bottle to my lips. I began to drink. Oops! Mistake number two. I'd never had alcohol before as I didn't like the way it smelt, nor was I curious enough to find out what it tasted like. "Mmmmm, this tastes good," I thought. This was such a surprise to me. It was like I was drinking a fizzy drink, and that wasn't what I expected alcohol to taste like at all. I sipped away at it as we talked, and it was over in what seemed like minutes. Lovely. I had another. And another. I was now starting to feel really great; I'd never experienced anything like it. Out of the corner of my eye, I could see that Hitler had given up on protesting and was enjoying a beer.

"After all," I could hear him reasoning, "Mum always let us have a drink at Christmas, so I'm sure she won't mind if we have it a little early." They all called her 'Mum' which she liked, and Hitler was right. She always offered them a drink at Christmas. I grabbed another cute bottle, this time a Cherry B. Mistake number three was that I began to drink it.

"Well well well," I thought. I had no idea that a drink could taste like that. It was a smooth, fruity, mind blowing flavour. It tasted amazing, and it was time for another one. This one I sipped, and I became aware that I was laughing for no reason. Just laughing. It was as if everything on the outside had been turned down a notch and was hazy and unimportant, and all that mattered was how I felt on the inside. A few others started laughing, and we all laughed our heads off. For no reason whatsoever. My tummy started to hurt because I'd laughed so much, and I needed to go to the loo. I stood up and, suddenly, the floor came up to me and smacked me in my face. There was total silence. I turned over on the floor as I realised that I had literally collapsed in a heap when I had risen from the chair. And I laughed again, loud and raucous, totally without restraint.

"How much did she have to drink?" Hitler asked, "cos she's totally drunk!" I listened to what he was saying intently and started laughing again. People around me thought that I was hilarious and started laughing too, while Hitler hoisted me off the floor and propped me up in a chair. I slid down and hit my face again, in what seemed like slow motion. He looked at my sister who'd stopped laughing. She'd never seen me drink before and found it all a bit overwhelming. She stared at me for awhile and someone said it might be a good idea to put me to bed. Everyone had stopped drinking and was staring at me incredulously, as no-one had seen me drink before. I was legless. Discombobulated. A mess. As I laughed away, the mood changed, and Hitler and Watson pulled me up at either side and walked me slowly up the stairs to my bedroom. My sister followed and pulled off my slippers after the guys dumped me on the bed. Apparently, she was really worried the guys told me afterwards, as I was the sensible one who never got into any real trouble. She was also probably worried because she'd have to do all the explaining to Mum. She was the eldest and would get the most flack, that's just how it was. My younger sister was asleep in the other bed in the room, and she woke up because of all the noise. I carried on laughing as she looked on curiously for awhile. I could see her trying to work out what was going on, but she didn't get it. It was late, she was tired, and she decided to carry on sleeping throughout all that was to come.

Suddenly, I realised that I didn't feel that great. The room had started to spin out of control, while I lay on a bed that did not want to keep still. Heaving and thrashing seemed to be taking place even though on some level, I realised I lay quietly on the bed – not moving. I didn't like the feelings that were coming at me in waves, but I couldn't do anything about it. I had no control over what was happening to me and I was scared shitless! My breath was coming faster and faster and I felt like I was crashing again, again, and again, like a boat on a sea of turmoil, which turned out to be my bed. Orff, orff, orff, went the feeling each time it crashed against whatever it was that was swirling around inside me. I didn't feel good anymore and I started to groan. I wanted things to stand still and I wanted things to be as they were before I started drinking – where was God when you needed him? Obviously not paying attention to me, as it got worse. I started flaying my arms about and making strange sounds which was too much for my sister, who burst into tears. Seeing her cry frightened me even more. "Why can't she understand me?" I thought. Then, everything changed.

I suddenly felt enclosed, like I was trapped in a void and I couldn't get out. I pounded, pushed and shoved, but I just couldn't escape. It was then that I felt the numbness. It started at my feet and was slowly spreading upwards. I became aware that I couldn't feel my feet or my ankles anymore and as I looked down, I saw nothing, as they were gone, just inky blackness enveloping my legs. I was numb with fear, as I watched my thighs disappear, gone into the black. I held my hands up in front of my eyes, turning them back and forth, looking at the oily darkness as it slowly crept up my arms and up my chest to my neck. The numbness was complete throughout my body and I was petrified that it would erase me, as if I never existed. "Oh Jesus, let me live," I thought, "I'm just a kid with so much to do. Pleassssse, I don't want to die." I wailed in my head.

The darkness came, up past my lips and I couldn't talk. It was as if my mouth no longer existed. I couldn't see beyond the cocoon of blackness that continued to engulf me, to coil around me and consume me. I didn't know what to do. I was screaming for help but no on could see or hear me. Yet there they were. All of them in my bedroom now that my sister was crying. I realised that I was praying to get through the night. I was doing deals with God, hoping that he would feel sorry for me and throw me a pass, so that I could be released from this madness. In the end, I promised that I'd never drink again. Ever. No more swearing I said, and no more eating out the biscuits after everyone had gone to sleep – letting my siblings take the blame. Never again. "Help me, please help me," was all I could say as the darkness swallowed me up completely, and then, I was gone. There was nothing, I was nothing, and I remained locked in that state for what seemed like forever.

The term 'God is good' formed in my mind as eventually, I was jolted back into the present and re-formed. I settled into my body and felt the warmth spreading through my veins as a mist started to lift. I turned over onto my side and vermilion bile spewed out of me. So forceful, that it came through my lips, my nose and would have bulged out of my eye sockets had the balls not been there. I was heaving and vomiting all over the floor. Huge amounts of stuff continued to come out of me, red and nasty and . . . such a relief!

When my sister calmed down, she took me to the bathroom to clean me up a little. The boys grabbed buckets, cloths and water and cleaned up the mess until the carpet looked pretty good, as most of the vomit was gone. The stench couldn't be erased, and tons of my Mums' favourite perfume was used to mask the rank odour. It didn't get rid of it completely, but things certainly smelled better. I then decided to try to escape from my bed, determined to get flowers from the garden to make the room smell okay. But, I was having a little trouble communicating, especially as our garden only contained weeds. Everything that I said came out as rubbish, and I started waving my arms and legs all over the place, without any real coordination. When I wasn't bleating on about flowers, I was swiping my nose, as it bled like it hadn't done before. It streamed out, thick and lava red, full of purpose and direction, tumbling from both nostrils. I could barely feel it, but It looked disgusting Hitler told me later. "We were thinking about calling an ambulance, as you seemed like you were demented, like you'd lost your mind," he said.

"I probably had," I thought. Eventually, they were able to get both me, and the nosebleed under control. They pinned me down and stuffed my nose with toilet paper which did the trick. And after awhile, I lay down, and decided to go to sleep.

I woke up, and remembered some of the night so far and the nonsense that I'd put them through was burned into my mind. I'd never felt so ashamed. Alcohol, it seemed, was not meant for me. As my mind continued to wander, I noticed that something was a little off. It was as if I couldn't control myself. My thoughts were not my own anymore and my mind seemed to be all over the place, out of order, out of action. "What the hell!" I thought. "After all that vomit and blood, I'm still flipping drunk? – or am I?"

I could see my sister curled up in the corner of the room crying and rocking herself perhaps for comfort? Watson was still scrubbing frantically at the carpet which wasn't quite as clean as he thought it could be. Bird stood in another corner of the room, looking on, waiting to be told what to do. Colin was downstairs clearing away the empty cans, bottles and cigarettes from our little session. He called out to Bird to give him a hand and, he obliged, no doubt happy to get out of the bedroom and to have something to do. As usual, Hitler took charge and asked my sister to give me a proper wash and get me into my night clothes as I'd thrown up on my outfit, and I looked like a crumpled wreck and smelt bad. My sister got it together and helped me to get up and into the bathroom.

I was calm on the outside, but I still had demons racing away inside my head. Questions came up in my mind about the meaning of life, about universal problems, about improbable and impossible math and its impact on our world, about historical fact and whether they were truths or just the rants or tales coming from great orators of their time . . . I struggled away with my thoughts as Sandra managed to pull my top off. She soaped a flannel to wash my hands and face and looked at me as if she was wondering where to start. She started with my hands and I gave no resistance as I was too busy thinking. She then turned me around to tackle the zip in my top. My mind had shifted to wonder what happens when we die? What happened to the bit of us that loves and cries and feels all that life has to offer? Hmmm. . . I thought about it for awhile, while Sandra picked pieces of vomit out of my hair and then pulled on my nightdress. My mind shifted and I asked myself if I was dead or alive . . . My mind went blank, unable to answer the question. What the hell was wrong with me? With my mind? I felt different, detached, as if I was watching myself from above, observing the scene while it played itself out, but still attached to my sister through an invisible string. A string? Or was it a thread . . . What the fuck! Sorry God for swearing yet again.

My mind was filling with questions that needed answering and I was starting to panic as I didn't have the answers, the knowledge, the wisdom to get . . . what? My breath came in short puffs, faster and faster. As the turmoil continued to rise inside of me, my sister stopped fussing my clothes and became still. She'd noticed, or sensed, that something was wrong. She swung me round and saw the tears in my eyes and that I was struggling, stuttering to form words that I couldn't quite release. She pulled me towards her and hugged me. It felt a bit strange at first and I resisted, but she wouldn't let me go. After awhile, and without warning, a floodgate opened, and I exploded with tears. I think she actually cried with me as we clung to each other for a moment. Her touch was enough to sooth me, giving me the strength to quieten the storm that was raging inside me. I sighed as the calm continued and I came back from that awkward place in my mind. Eventually, I stopped crying, and we released from our embrace. We laughed self-consciously and she patted my shoulder. I felt air entering my body and I could breathe again. Normality had returned. "Jeez, that was close," I thought. She helped me to finish up in the bathroom and back into the bedroom, and as I lay down on my bed, I whispered, "thank you," very quietly. She pulled up my blanket and straightening the covers she replied,

"Don't ever drink again, it's not for you." Out went the light and I followed suit. When my Mum came home, everything was spotless, and the boys had gone.

The next day, the only evidence of our shenanigans was my swollen face from the fall the night before. My Mum never asked me about it – and I never brought it up. I felt awful, but I was so happy to be alive that I totally ignored the hammers pounding away in my head. My eyes were puffy, and my nose still had tissue stuck up each nostril, and while I knew that I looked a mess, I couldn't understand why I was feeling so bad. I asked my sister if there was something wrong with me as I felt worse as the day wore on. I mean, what the hell was going on? I didn't have a cold or the flu, even though I felt like I'd been knocked about in a fight and lost. So, what was it? I drank yet another glass of water but couldn't seem to quench my thirst. And why was I sweating? It wasn't even hot! I was starting to think that I had some sort of terminal illness, and then my sister put me straight. "It's called a hangover," she diagnosed, as she helped me pulled the tissue out of my nostrils and tried to make me look half decent. I hung around with her for awhile, while we rinsed out my clothes which were coated with blood and alcohol from the night before. I hung them out to dry once we'd worked out all the stains. "It's just what happens when you drink too much," was all she said.

"Are you kidding me? Is this what people felt like when they partied and got hammered?" I thought incredulously. I just couldn't get my head around it, so I didn't try. All I knew was that drinking wasn't for me and that I wasn't gonna touch alcohol again in a hurry. I was so glad to be alive and on the other side of being drunk that I ended up having the best day ever, despite the hangover.

The guys pooled their money together and were able to buy back the bottles and cans that we'd drunk from the Christmas stash. None of us ever mentioned that night again after that. It was a crazy evening that I suspected that we all wanted to forget.

When my Mum offered the boys their usual Christmas drink a few weeks later, all of them said emphatically, "NO THANK YOU." She was amazed, but didn't push it.

"More for me," she said.

Fifteen – At the party again . . .

I once again zapped out of my memories and jolted back into the present. In the background, the music had slowed. I could hear Delroy Wilson singing his broken heart out, "I'm still waiting . . . and with every little beat of my heart girl, I'm under your spell . . ." he sang in a sorrowful, but sensual way. In a way that told you that he was waiting for his girl – because she was special. Every one of us that listened to that record, every girl, wanted to be Delroy Wilson's girl. He was coming to the end of the song, ". . . I need your love so desperately," he sang, and, on this occasion, I didn't melt. In fact, I was only listening with half an ear because I was too busy reflecting on how many memories I had stored around illness. I felt as if I was trapped, held hostage in the bathroom. I was missing out on the party of the century, thinking back over my childhood. Thinking about things and times that were long forgotten — for a reason. I desperately wanted to join the party, to be a carefree teenager, singing along to my favourite music while having fun. But that wasn't happening. Instead, I was once again being given time out. To tend to myself, to focus on myself, because of illness. Once again, the sadness and loneliness descended like a fog over me. I felt old and forgotten, left to my own devices to deal with my nosebleeds and my thoughts. My problems.

'Black Woman, oh Black woman, you get the heaviest loads . . .' sang Judy Mowatt in the background, as I realised that I'd spent the last couple of hours going over all those memories, when I usually only focus on what's happening right in front of me. In the here and now. But tonight, was different as I'd never scrutinised those incidents so closely before. I'd actually never given many of them any thought at all. They seemed like they were all so long ago . . . But suddenly, in one evening, they had all come tumbling out, running freely from my mind and escaping like the blood that poured out of me, time and time again. As I stared into space, I stopped myself from feeling overwhelmed, telling myself that I could handle it, "it's all part of me, so it's all good," I said. I looked into my past once again, really looking. I mean, what else was there to do, stuck in the bathroom that had become my second home.

I began to see links and patterns; I began to see some sort of order. Fighting through measles, through school, for my space in the family, for my space in the world, for control over my body. Always fighting something or someone. As I thought about that revelation some more, I liked it. I'd never seen that about myself. A slow smile spread across my face, as I warmed to myself and filled up with a sense of pride. It occurred to me that I'd spent hours trawling through my memories and that most of it made me feel sad about myself. But not anymore. I was a fighter I realised, which meant that I'd never give up; had stamina; was a warrior. I liked that about myself a lot and was feeling on a high – until I remembered the alcohol incident.

Being drunk was, without a doubt, my moment of shame. I felt so embarrassed at how totally I'd fallen apart. I was also scared shitless by the whole mind-bending thing that came with being hammered. I shuddered to shake off the images that flashed across my mind. I definitely wasn't built to take on alcohol – or for that matter drugs – as I soon realised when I visited one of my school friends a few months before. This led me into yet another uncomfortable memory which had been flitting around in my mind, darting here and there, like a moth keeps flying to the light. Finally, it had landed.

***

She was a transfer kid that came to my school when she was thirteen, and she was different. Maria had a sense of danger and daring that I was unfamiliar with and a confidence that I hadn't seen before. Also, she wasn't local, and she didn't have the Hackney vibe. But, she didn't feel like she was from south London either, where it was so weird, with a tension that Hackney didn't have – where people were more on edge. I remember when I must have been about eight or nine, and my Mum took me to a market in Peckham. It was the fastest shop that she ever did, as she couldn't wait to get back to Hackney.

She said, "I can't put my finger on why but, mi na like it over this side t'all." I knew what she meant as, even as a kid, I had felt it too. It was like meeting people that looked and sounded like you, but felt like they were from a different planet. Maria didn't feel like she was from any part of London. I just couldn't get a handle on her – but we clicked. She seemed more experienced, more worldly wise than most of the teenagers that I hung around with, like she'd been around the block a few times. I liked that.

After a few weeks we got talking, and an odd, but interesting friendship began to develop. She was smart but didn't really get a lot of the lessons that we were working on, so I suggested that we could study together, which we did after school. It was strange as it was one of my first real friendships in school, but she seemed to like me, and so I went with it.

Sometimes she would invite me over to her house to study, which was a revelation and like stepping into another world. She lived in Holly Street Estate, which was something that I'd never encountered. I remember the first time that I went into the estate, I was aware of how 'wrong' the whole place felt. It was a labyrinth of internal corridors shaped in a rectangular style estate that felt almost like it was underground, another world, its own planet. It was one of those places that must have looked amazing when it was just an idea but wasn't great in reality. The word that came into my mind when I rode the lift to her flat was oppressive. All the flats in her block were housed in long corridors, all contained and covered, without windows or gaps to let the outside world in. They ran the entire length of the estate, with each flat having a dingy coloured door in the murky hallway. It was the kind of place that made you want to look behind you when you walked. Looking for what I don't know, but looking, nonetheless. Her flat was a maisonette with the kitchen on the top level and all the other rooms downstairs, which she shared with her mum, and her sister, who was five years older than her. The whole flat felt claustrophobic and confined, in a way that I'd never encountered before. I know I shouldn't have criticised where she lived, as I'd always lived-in council housing myself – but this place? It was on another level. It had brown and orange décor, which was really fashionable and, the furniture was the same as in all the houses that I'd ever visited or lived in. But, there was something about the place that made me feel trapped, as I sat in her kitchen, weighed down in a way that I'd never felt in anyone's place before.

Maybe it had something to do with the design of the estate, as I later knew other people who lived in Holly Street, and their flats looked, felt and smelt exactly the same. I sat in her kitchen, waiting in silence while she quickly collected some books, and I listened to her empty home. I could hear a television; a baby crying; music; and an argument; all happening at the same time. All with the muteness that comes from semi sound outside of your home. It was low level white noise which I found intrusive, and I couldn't wait to leave her maisonette, her estate, her life, and breathe some fresh air. It was always the same when I visited. The corridors into her flat would stink – mostly with curry, cabbage, rubbish, or something else that I couldn't identify –

and, as I left, I would breathe a sigh of relief. I would only spend short bursts of time at Maria's, I would never go there on my own, after dark.

Her mum was a typical mum, always trying to feed me, even though I wasn't really a fan of english cooking, and her sister Lana, was off the chart. I'd observed that mix race kids usually came in two packages – the 'I'm really good looking' package or the 'I'm really not that good looking' package. There didn't seem to be an 'in-between' option. Harsh, but true. Lana was well up there on the looks side of things.

Maria was okay looking too, with a five-inch really curly brown afro, spot free skin, a decent shape and of average height. Lana, on the other hand was tall, with glowing skin, long straight shiny brown hair and the face of an angel. The first time I met her, I just kept staring. I mean, people who looked like her were a rarity in my world. They were on billboards and in magazines, and didn't live in Holly Street Estate, normally. She looked so glamorous and polished as she got ready for work that I was convinced she was a model. When I asked Maria what she did, she said that her sister was a croupier in a West End casino. And even though I didn't know what that was, I guessed it was a good thing, a posh thing. Lana had the confidence that came with beauty, but she was not arrogant with it. She was so comfortable to be around, just like any other ordinary girl. While she got ready for work, we would chat, and giggle and she even let us try on her make-up. I gave it a go, and quickly took it off as I saw that I looked like CoCo the clown when I glanced in the mirror. Maria looked good in makeup, had the same confidence as Lana to a degree, but she was more ordinary than confident and seemed more laid back than her sister. Maria's mum was pretty lax with her I thought. Hell, Maria even managed to throw in a swear word or two when she and her mum argued. Like I said, it was a different world, definitely not what I was used to, and I was fascinated – but always glad to be home after a stint at Maria's.

I remember being so envious of Maria's casualness towards all things school, and her lack of respect for our teachers was something that I couldn't get my head around. "Didn't all teachers deserve our respect?" I once questioned, pausing as we worked through a particularly tricky algebra problem at school.

"Nope," said Maria. "Only the good ones."

"But they know what they're talking about, so shouldn't we listen?" I insisted.

"Er. . . nope," said Maria as she pretended to think. She looked at me like I was dumb. "Just because someone is talking, it doesn't mean that you have to listen."

Hmmm. That was a new concept to me. I imagined saying that to my Mum. And I also imagined the response would be a slap upside my head, a year's worth of being grounded followed by a healthy dose of cussing and shouting. Maria on the other hand had a less structured, hands-off upbringing. I admired it to a degree, but it also meant that I was constantly being challenged by her way of thinking and attitude to life. She was a dare devil, hands on, try everything and anything girl. And I was not. Needless to say, as Maria settled into school and got to know her way around the area, our friendship became more muted and eventually died. She cared less about school and more about having a 'good time', and eventually dropped out of school at fourteen.

I didn't give Maria another thought for ages, until my school friend Annie mentioned that Maria had had a baby and that she was thinking about going to visit her. "Whoa there," I said to Annie. "Back it up! When did this happen?"

"Seems like she'd dropped out of school way back, met this loser Turkish boy, and the rest was history," said Annie. I stared at her in shock until she said, "stop staring and shut your mouth – you look like a goldfish!" My eyebrows were way up into my hairline and I continued to stare. "What? I'm just telling it like I heard it . . ." she finished. She told me that their mums knew each other, and that was why she was up to date on Maria's news.

"Oh . . ." was all I said, still in shock. Annie explained that she really wanted to catch up with Maria but was too nervous to go alone. She knew that we'd been friends so, we arranged that we'd meet up, and go visit her together. Later, on my way home from school, I found myself thinking, "really? pregnant at fifteen? REALLY?" I thought she'd be different, better than us somehow. One of those girls that would do great things, like her sister – because of how she was, because of how she looked. I knew that I was being unreasonable as we were all just kids but, I thought that she was special, a badass. And, it turned out that she wasn't.

At first glance, she looked the same, and so did everything else – same estate same smells. But it was different. Maria looked like she was as surprised as we were that she had ended up in such a predicament. I sneaked a proper look at her once we'd hugged and I'd seen the baby. That girl had changed completely as she was swollen, sullen and wasn't as pretty as she once was. Nor was she as confident and cocky as I'd remembered. I'd walked into Holly Street Estate and back into Maria's life for the first time in ages, and I instantly became depressed. Why? Because it wasn't the kind of place that you'd want to be living in when you're fifteen, and a young mum. It had the same dingy lighting and loud noises and still looked shabby as hell. Don't get me wrong, I wasn't that kid that judged other people, as my life was just as hard, as we struggled to get by in a single parent household. It's just that Holly Street wasn't the place where Maria, or any kid, could feel like they'd made a success of their life. It wasn't fair to think that, but I couldn't help it. I was disappointed in her. It was like her journey, her future, had come crashing to a halt. It was obviously not where she thought she would end up, and it showed. She had nothing to say and neither did I – other than "your baby looks cute." I mean, what could I say?

"Why was this all so . . . awkward, difficult?" I asked myself as I scanned the kitchen that was exactly the same. "I'd looked up to her I suppose, as she had an ease and a self-awareness that I knew I lacked. She was beautiful and had everything going for her," was my answer. But as I stared at her on that day, I just couldn't relate to the whole grown-up-ness that was now her life. I mean, everything looked chaotic. Nappies, baby clothes, stuff for bottles and more baby clothes were strewn all over the over-cramped, suffocating flat. Her fella was around when we turned up, and they looked as if they were in the middle of something tense as we eased into the living room. We could hear them arguing in the kitchen upstairs. Apparently, he'd promised to be more hands-on and, she needed more money for even more baby stuff. He grunted something out, and she whined for a bit longer. Back and forth it went while Annie and I sat there looking at their baby, pretending not to hear what was going on. Eventually she came downstairs after the front door slammed shut. "Sorry about that," she said as she smoothed her dress and quickly checked on the baby. She was pissed at him, I could tell. I'd seen that look many times when my Mum was at the end of one of her dodgy relationships.

Jesus! It was all too scary. I mean, she was acting as if she was a grown up, with grown up worries and expressions. But how could that be? We were still kids. We were still going to school and being told what to do by our parents – well that was the case for Annie and me. We were still being given pocket money (if we were lucky) and coming home to dinner cooked by our mums. So, how could Maria now have a kid and be acting like she had been with this guy for the last ten years? As I sat there, taking in the sheer volume of stuff that this tiny child demanded, it came to me that Maria was in a different league to us. I'd lost a friend, and was looking at this kid, who was playing at being a grown up. I felt betrayed, hurt that she'd let things play out that way. What a waste. She was meant to do great things, be a great person, and now, she was just . . . ordinary.

Maria decided that she needed a smoke which was fine by me as I wanted to do something, anything, to normalise the awkward situation, and we went up to the kitchen, as the baby was sleeping. She started to roll a spliff and before I could digest what she was actually doing, she lit up and blew out a plume of hazy smoke. Annie had a drag, and not to be outdone, I also pulled on it hard and we sat there smoking and, suddenly talking. Maria put some music on, and we laughed, I mean really laughed, and remembered old times. She didn't seem to want to talk about her predicament and to be honest, we didn't want to hear. So, time passed, and then it was our cue to leave, with kisses and promises to return. As I walked down the corridor towards the stairs – side stepping the lift, which was out of order – I knew that I had to leave Maria behind. I knew I wouldn't be seeing her again. So, I left Holly Street Estate with Annie without looking back, walking down a long road where buses didn't seem to want to travel, to the bus stop which was fifteen minutes away.

By the way, it'd been the first time that I'd ever smoked weed (I may have forgotten to mention), and while I tried to keep it together, I was freaking out on the inside. I felt so alive and everything had become heightened to the point that was scary.

Colour was vivid, sound was melodic, and I felt like I was feeling anything and everything for the first time. I could feel my body, my breathing, my heart, air on my skin – it was amazing. I was glowing, literally, and I could see a halo of light around Annie and everyone that walked past us. Some halos burned brighter than others and I was intrigued. I squinted and probably over-stared at people and I even passed a few trees and noticed that they also had a hue, a glow. And then I looked at Annie to see where she was with it all. She didn't look back at me, because she was concentrating on the broken pavements and dodging the doggy poop that seem to be everywhere.

But I could feel her. I could feel that we were connected, and I could feel . . . shit, wait . . .

What the hell could I feel?

Wait what???

This was not what I was supposed to feel. Suddenly, I could tell that she liked me, I mean really, really liked me in an intense and excited way. How I identified her feelings was odd as I'd never felt anything like it before – ever. But I intuitively knew what it was. It was raw, and . . . not the sort of thing that I wanted to feel at all. It was coming towards me in waves, cloaking me, killing my vibe and squashing my high. It scared the living daylights out of me. I knew what it was to be gay and I understood that women could feel like that too. So, in the absence of any experience of 'those' sort of feelings, I panicked. "Was this what it feels like?" I wondered silently, as I walked with my friend in what I hoped was a straight line. "Is this what love feels like? Is that why my heart is beating so fast? Jeez, did this mean that I was gay?" I asked myself all these questions and a ton more. I'd never experienced anything like it before and while I was freaking out, there was something else. It was kinda nice to have someone feeling good feelings about me. I could sense her vibrations, flowing over the airways, bridging the gap between us as we walked. I couldn't believe that she was throwing herself right at me. Slapping me in the face and exposing me to what? Loud and clear, in a language that only she and I knew.

Not a word had been spoken as we continued to walk. We were exactly the same people that went to see Maria, which had been a trauma in itself, leaving me filled with much sorrow as I watched her feeding her child. And now, there was Annie, throwing her shit my way. As I intuitively knew what she was feeling, I also knew that she was allowing me to see a side of herself that was hidden, until now. Our encounter with weed had helped to expose her secret. She couldn't hide from me anymore. She liked me, more than a friend, and she like girls and not boys. My certainty was ridiculous, but it was there.

It was a noisy evening on a busy road in Hackney. People jostled and walked fast, cars sped past, and the smell of the city changed. Fish and chips, pizza and Wimpy smells filled the air and there was a pub at every junction waiting for its customers. Night-time in Hackney was arriving. That's when things came to life and the energy changed. All of this was lost on me though. It was as if Annie and I were contained in a bubble which muted everything around us. The sight, smells and sounds were missing. It was just us.

As we walked, my energy changed. "This wasn't the Annie that I knew," I thought. We'd spent so much time together, laughing and joking and having fun at school. But this silent feeling between us changed everything. I was no longer feeling flattered or special, but sad. It welled up from nowhere and swirled around me. "Don't cry girl, please don't cry," I said to myself over and over again. That's when I could feel that a headache was building, gnawing away at the remnants of my buzz. I was overwhelmed and just needed to escape. We were coming up to a junction where buses ran and suddenly, I didn't want to walk anymore. I needed to go home and get away from the feelings that Annie was flowing at me. She still hadn't looked at me since leaving Maria's, which was odd, and she didn't look at me when I suddenly said that I was taking a different route. She just kept staring at the pavement, her eyes glued to the ground. "Oh, there's my bus, bye," I said looking back as I started to run towards the bus stop. At that moment she looked up to answer and I was stunned by the look of sheer misery on her face. I turned back to her and gave her a quick hug, which was our standard greeting. She didn't say a word. "Jesus," I thought, "get me out of here!" I ran for the bus, even though I had obviously missed it, and waited for the next one to arrive.

I sat on the top deck which was thankfully empty and leaned my cornrowed head on the window. I finally let my tears fall because I knew that I had lost not one, but two friends that night.

Maria was not such a blow as we were no longer close. I think that it was more that I was sorry for her situation. I came away from her new life knowing that I was never going to go down that route. Not only that, she looked so unhappy, with everything. They all had that same look – surprised. No way. All that 'nappies, bottles and arguments with your man shit' was not for me. I hadn't ever had a boyfriend and, after seeing her slice of life, I didn't want one. Not like hers anyway. I was slightly pissed off with myself as I'd always looked up to her, as I thought she was special. And now? I didn't. There were so many girls of my age who were having babies, that it wasn't even scandalous anymore. Why would they do it, I wondered. We all knew about sex, kinda, and we knew about the pill and condoms and stuff. So why? I just couldn't get it. I wiped the window that I was leaning on, so that I could get a better view of outside as I didn't want to miss my stop. As I looked up, I saw that an older woman was staring at me, she had a tissue in her hand and leaned towards me.

"Thank you," I said as I took the tissue and blew my nose.

"Don't worry yourself chile, things going to get better – you watch and see!" I smiled a watery smile and turned my head to look out of the window.

"I didn't get Annie either. How could I have not known?" I asked myself. It didn't occur to me that I may have got it wrong. That I may have got her wrong. I mean, one spliff didn't make me a psychic, I knew that. But, I knew she was gay, just like I knew I was not. As my journey on the bus came to an end, I wiped my face, but I couldn't do anything about my eyes that were as red as a stop sign. I then squared my shoulders, and I headed home.

Luckily, everyone was in the living room watching a movie in the dark, so I was able to sneak in and blend. I stared at the television screen for ages not taking in what was on. I just sat there, staring, unable to think, unable to do, high as a kite right under my Mum's nose. If she knew she would kill me. Then bring me back to life, and then kill me again. Taking drugs to her was, "serious business," as she liked to say, and she had zero tolerance. Interestingly, she didn't count weed as too much off limits, as it grew in the back garden when she lived in Trinidad. Everyone grew it as it had many uses; you could drink it, smoke it, use it as a poultice and eat it for different ailments. But, being high at my age, whether it was through weed, drink or anything else, was a no no as far as she was concerned.

Later that night, as I lay in bed thinking things through with Custard Cream biscuits that I'd stolen from the kitchen, I couldn't come up with a plan on how to deal with Annie. I munched my way through half the packet and tried to focus. I still had a low-level buzz and felt overwhelmed, as everything seemed insurmountable. I was also uncomfortable because of the crumbs that now lived in my bed. I could feel them against my skin like a carrot on a grater, and I started to itch. I scratched and lost my train of thought for awhile. I couldn't get my blanket to cover my toes and I wiggled around, trying to make it happen. That made the itching worse and the cycle began again. I went through two rotations of itch, scratch, wiggle, and when I couldn't stand it any longer, I flung myself out of bed and dusted off the crumbs. In truth there wasn't much to dust out – even though it felt like I was sleeping in a sandpit – but it made me feel better. I remade the bed and settled back in, snuggling under the covers, as my thoughts returned.

I was fifteen for goodness sake, so how was I supposed to solve something like this. And, I had to admit that I liked the feelings that I felt, the whole physical nature of it. It was so . . . exciting.

But these feelings weren't supposed to happen with a girl – were they?

I was supposed to feel this way with boys, – wasn't I?

I was so conflicted and confused that I could feel it spiralling out of control, and being high just made it one hundred times worse. I thought I was going mad with uncontrollable thoughts going round and around in my head. Annies' problem had become my problem, and . . . what was her problem again?

Did I like her like that?

Maybe if I looked deeper I could . . . what?

What was I, a lesbian? I munched another biscuit.

How, yes how would I know . . .? Whoops! I think I've lost the plot – and my biscuit! I itched, and then I scratched. I found and nibbled my biscuit as I tried to make it all slow down. My thoughts were coming all at once, way too fast for me to keep up. I wiggled in my bed as my heart raced and my breath came in shallow jerks. And then, I promptly fell asleep.

I woke up in a bed full of crumbs and a mouth so parched that if felt as if cement had set around my teeth. My lips were so dry that they'd turned white, and it took awhile for me to remember what had happened the day before. I trembled as I hid the evidence of my feast and drank a gallon of water. "Jesus, is that what happens when you get high?" I thought. "Well, I won't be doing that again," I promised myself. As I washed and readied myself for school, it came back to me. I remembered how afraid I'd become, feeling like I was losing it. "What the hell," I thought, startled at how vivid last night's memory was, "I think I might have said a few prayers n' shit." I laughed at myself nervously for being such a baby, even though it had all felt soooo real. Wasn't that what I was supposed to do – laugh it off?

More memories came back to me in fragments as I raced through breakfast and sat on the bus on my way to school. I was hoping that I could blot out yesterday and put the whole thing behind me. Maybe rack it up as one of life's experiences that had gone wrong. But no. Memories came flooding back to me and I remembered my time with Annie, and cringed, and then sighed. As I still didn't have a plan on how to deal with her, I decided that the sensible thing to do was – to do nothing. I mean what actually happened? Nothing. Maybe it was all in my mind. I'd heard of people getting 'para' from taking drugs, getting confused about what was real and what wasn't. Was that me?

Maybe.

Probably.

No!

I knew what I felt was true and real. I knew that Annie was gay. The most common-sense thing to do would have been to ask her, but that was never gonna happen. I'd had enough drama to last me for a lifetime – real or imagined. First Maria, and then Annie. So no, I wasn't going to be bringing it up anytime soon.

There was also another underlying issue that I also didn't want to think about, which was that it could have been me that was gay, a lesbian, a dyke. I could barely say the words to myself because I felt uncomfortable. It didn't sit right with me. And it wouldn't sit right with anyone around me. Being black and 'girl on girl' was not an option in my family, or with anyone that I knew. Nothing had been said overtly, and I didn't know anyone who was gay, but it was there, nonetheless. Sometimes I'd catch a vibe in the dance hall music that I listened to. 'Batti man a dutti man', was the essence of what they said, and lesbians weren't even a thing, never mentioned – didn't exist. I didn't know enough about it or myself to answer the question of my sexuality. Hell, I hadn't ever felt anything like I had the night before. But my instinct told me that to talk about any of this with my sister or my family would bring a whole lot of trouble that I could do without. I knew that I would have to figure this out by myself. So what did I do about it? I went to school and carried on as if it was a normal day. I saw Annie as usual, and neither of us mentioned the night before, the being high bit, or the visit to Maria again.

***

I came back to the present with a bump as I realised that I'd manage to push the whole incident to the back of my mind for months, until now, at the party of a lifetime. Until now, because I'd been forced to stop and be still, thanks to the endlessness of this nosebleed. A natural pause moment had occurred, and I was suddenly able to untangle a muddle that I'd been unable to cope with at the time. I realised that I really missed my friendship with Annie and that I really didn't like girls in a physical kind of way – Michael had taught me that. I needed to fix things with her because I was no longer fearful of anything. I suddenly knew what I had to do to make things right. Annie was my friend and that – was that! In the background I picked up strains of 'One Nation Under a Groove' blaring out of the speakers upstairs and vaguely imagined the crazy dancing going on to Funkadelic's latest tune ". . . Getting down just for the funk of it, nothing can stop us now . . ." I sang along under my breath.

In the absence of nothing better to do, and with one hand on my nostrils, I decided to clean out the medicine cabinet, throwing away expired or unusable medicines and remedies. There was the usual crap in there for my emergencies as well as some bits and pieces. A half used blue dye sat in the corner, staining the cabinet a beautiful sky-blue where it had been abandoned, its muslin casing stuck to the surface like chewing gum on the bottom of my desk at school. That went. Next to it stood a bottle of smelling salts that was older than me probably, its label, worn and erased from constant use over the years. That stayed. On the bottom shelf there was a greasy, and therefore totally useless sticky plaster, a 'lifebuoy' soap, along with a 'mystery ointment' which smelt like something that could be rubbed onto a horse. It reminded me of what my mum smelt like when she had a backache, so I decided that it was useful, and I didn't chuck it in the bin. All the rest of the stuff that I came across was dumped. I stuffed tissue up both nostrils as a temporary stopper, and washed my hands, squinting at my image in the mirror as I smoothed my eyebrows.

In that moment it became clear to me that it might be a good idea not to do alcohol or drugs again, ever. I also realised that something had happened inside, and I could now admit that I really liked Michael. Lots. I kinda knew it before, but I was filled with doubt, and convinced myself that he couldn't be interested in me. But I didn't think that anymore. "I'm good enough," I thought optimistically. "It's just that I've screwed things up with the whole nosebleed thing, as usual," I said to myself, and I wasn't so hopeful anymore. I pulled out my stoppers, and my nose continued to drip blood into the sink.

It then dawned on me that I'd lost my moment, my window of opportunity. My kiss. And I was crushed. My mood had become pretty subdued because I'd been left to my own devices in the bathroom for way too long. I felt as though I was missing out on life, and it irked the hell out of me. "Irked the hell out of me – who even speaks like that?" I thought, and decided to be angry at my words, instead of the situation for a moment. In truth, I probably wasn't missing out on much at all, but I'd gotten to the point where I'd lost perspective. Everything that went wrong in my life was the fault of all things physical ailments. Life had wound me up and in turn, I'd coiled myself into an angry ball even more. Tears threatened to come again, but I brushed them aside.

"STOP!" I demanded of myself and my tears. "I decided. . . I've had enough of this shit."

Slowly, things began to calm down both inside my head and inside my nose. I was at the point where I could squeeze tightly, and hopefully stop the blood-flow. It was a precise operation and, I'd had years of experience. If I tried to apply pressure too soon, the blood would back-up and run down my throat instead. And I didn't want that.

I tentatively let go of my nose and waited.

And waited.

Nothing.

There's no two ways about it. Every time I had a nosebleed, we went on a journey, my blood and me. It changed me, released me. We'd get to know each other better. It was a time for me to stop, feel, and listen to my inner voice. And, now that I'd had a chance to trawl through all that helped to make me me, I think at last, I heard it

I breathed a sigh of relief, and gently, began to clean myself and the bathroom up as best I could. Luckily, my clothes were unaffected as I'd caught the flow early, and I didn't wear make-up so had nothing to worry about in that direction. I'd sluiced out the bath and was drying my hands when Stephanie came in and stopped at the sight of me. Although the bathroom was clean, the iron rich smell of blood still hung in the air. She could tell that something wasn't right, and I was mortified. She was a friend of my sisters who hung out with her at the weekends. They didn't go to the same school but had friends in common, so I didn't see her around much. She kept herself to herself and I'd hardly really spoken to her at all. She was a scrawny, dark skinned girl, with a sassy attitude, and I'd always admired her from a distance. She had a different way of thinking to the rest of the group and wasn't afraid to say her piece. I could tell that she thought about what she was saying before she opened her mouth, which in our group was a rarity. She had a confidence that I liked, and a very persuasive tongue. She would start off opposing everyone in the group when they talked, and by the end of it, she would have everyone on her side. In fact, she was so slick, I'd often wondered why she hung around with my sister and her friends at all. They never really challenged her. Maybe that's what she liked, never being challenged, I mean. Being queen of the castle perhaps. I couldn't work her out. She even had her own style. Because she was so slim, absolutely everything that she wore looked cool, hung beautifully. I loved the way she dressed, especially the shirt that she was wearing. I hadn't seen anything like it before, but I was too shy to tell her that I liked it.

"Sorry, I just wanted to wash my hands," she nodded towards the toilet door indicating that she'd just come out of there.

"Erm, okay, I was just finishing up" I said, embarrassed that such a cool girl had caught me at my most vulnerable moment. I just wanted to sneak out of the bathroom and go straight up to my room. The party was pretty much over for me, although judging by the sounds I could hear, it was showing no signs of winding down for everybody else. Louisa Marks was now blaring out of the speaker, the brassy baseline original and distinctive. I could hear the girls singing along with the lyrics ". . . I know you're having an affair. And I know who, and I know where . . ."

"Are you ok? Is this a bad time? It's just that you have a little blood on the side of your face. . ." she continued as she hovered at the entrance. I could tell that she was curious about the blood and I decided to blurt it out.

"I've had a massive nosebleed that's been going on for hours," I snapped. I sighed wearily, as I wanted to go to bed and forget this night had ever happened.

"Do you have nosebleeds?" she asked incredulously. "Oh my god – so do I," she laughed out loud and kept saying, "oh my god, oh my god."

"What's so funny?" I asked irritably. I was only listening to her with half an ear and I was starting to think that maybe, just maybe, she wasn't so cool after all.

"I had one just as I was about to come to the party." I looked at her blankly. "You know," she continued smiling, "a nosebleed. They always happen at the wrong time," she grinned at me excitedly, and then, I smiled. She was right. They always happened at the wrong time.

"I don't know anyone that has nosebleeds – except me, said Stephanie. "It's such a nightmare. I've always hated them, apart for today cos it's given me a reason to talk to you. I've wanted to speak to you for ages."

"Me? You wanted to speak to me?" I stared at her dumbstruck.

"Yeah," she continued, "you're way calmer than your sister and her friends. They can be a little . . ."

"Crazy loud?" I finished for her. We both smiled. It seemed as if we had more in common than I originally guessed. "I always thought you were down with all that." I explained, "I mean, you guys hang out most weekends."

"Not really. I suppose that cos I grew up with some of the girls, I got into the habit of hanging around with them, is all." She smiled sheepishly, "to be honest they've been getting on my nerves lately, all they want to talk about is man. That's not me." She straightened her clothes a little, even though they looked perfectly fine to me.

"That's not me either," I said. I paused and sighed unconsciously. "I hate my life right now, as I've spent most of the night in here," I grumbled, as I finished tidying the bathroom. In truth, the bathroom was fine, it was just that I was nervous about going back to the party and I was looking for something to delay the inevitable. My nose was completely fine, and all was back to normal. Except, I couldn't forget what an idiot I'd been when my nose had started to bleed. I ran off like Cinderella, when the clock struck twelve. Except I hadn't left a glass slipper, I'd left a trail of blood. Ok, perhaps not a trail of blood, but you get my drift. It was embarrassing!

"Well, I wish I could have your life right now," Stephanie said, grinning from ear to ear. I was bemused that she'd want to have my life. I looked at her and she looked at me. I looked at her some more and she looked right back at me. "What the hell is wrong with this girl?" I thought.

"He's still outside," she said finally as I continued to stare at her in a vacant way. She could tell that the information meant nothing as I was shrugging my shoulders, indicating that I had no idea what she was talking about. "He must really like you, is all I'm saying." This was met with another blank look from me.

"Jesus, I need to get away from her. She's really starting to piss me off with all her riddles, I haven't got time for this," I thought

"He asked me to check on you – he didn't want to embarrass you by coming in himself," she whispered discretely. Finally, the penny dropped.

"Ohhhhh, you mean Michael?" I questioned incredulously. "Had he been outside the bathroom, waiting for me to come back out?" I wondered.

Stephanie must have guessed my thoughts as she said, "yep, he's been waiting outside all this time. I've been to get at least four drinks and a piece of chicken and he's just been hanging out down here. I had no idea why he wasn't upstairs dancing, but I guess I know the reason why, now." It was one of those moments that it was good to be black, so that I could hide the blush that had crept onto my cheeks. It didn't matter as she could tell that I was both embarrassed and pleased at the same time. "You guys really fit well together," she observed. "Everyone thinks he's this outgoing guy who's a 'ladies' man, but he's really quiet."

"Really?" was what I said. "How do you know so much about him?" was what I was thinking – suspiciously. It was starting to dawn on me that she might know him just a little too damn well. Perhaps because she had already dated him? Once again, she read my mind.

"Oh no, nothing like that," she laughed, putting up her hands as if to ward off something evil. "He's my cousin." I breathed a sigh of relief and relaxed once again. I had no idea that I'd been holding my breath, and how important that answer had been, until then. "He's a really sweet guy, who just happens to be deliciously good looking," she added slyly, just to make me blush again. It worked. "He swears that he's stopped chasing skirt and he's been banging on about you for weeks. He thought you were too nice to want to go out with someone like him."

"Really?" was all I said, while on the inside, my tummy was doing somersaults. I thought I was the only one with insecurities, but obviously not. I put Stephanie straight right away, and even let on that I only hung around with Sandra and her mates because I had to. It was her turn to say, "really?" and then she asked me to explain.

I told her that my Mum was pretty open minded about us going out, and was cool about us being out until quite late. The only rule was that we had to go out together and that we had to come back together. Now, that kinda worked for me as I didn't really go out. I was happy to hang out at home and read and draw and just chill. Not so for my sister. If she wasn't out, then she wasn't alive. She lived on the street and because of this, so did I. It was an uneasy relationship which over time had become more strained. I just didn't want to hang out with her and her friends anymore, but she made it really difficult for me to say no. She'd pick an argument, hide things and sometimes destroy my stuff to get her own way, and, just to keep the peace, I'd put up with it. Over the last week though, I'd refused to hang around with her anymore, which meant that tensions were high between me, her and her entourage.

"It all makes sense now," said Stephanie "Michael wasn't so sure about you because you were always with that group, but I put him straight." At my look of concern, she quickly continued, "I mean, I told him that you weren't like them, and now I understand why." I shot her a grateful look. "I'm glad I spoke up for you," she finished.

Even as I broke into a smile at the unbelievable turn of events, I was still hesitant to go back and join what was left of the party. I felt incredibly shy all of a sudden as I had never been seen as an individual before, I'd always been in the background and part of the crowd. Yet, here I was, with not one, but potentially two friends all at once. "What are you waiting for?" asked Stephanie. She was right of course, what was I waiting for.

"Nothing." I said, and I shuffled past Stephanie and walked into the hall.

Michael was waiting outside as predicted by Stephanie, and his attention quickly turned to me as he saw me leave the bathroom.

"Feeling better?" He asked, looking at me with concerned eyes. I nodded dumbly. We just stared at each other for a while. "Dance?" He asked. Again, I just nodded like an idiot and followed him upstairs into the living room.

I had to adjust to the noise and the atmosphere. Quite a few people had left, however there was more than enough people present to keep the vibe nice. The DJ had slowed things down and it was mostly couples slow dancing, enjoying the sultry sounds of Sugar Minott. We slid into the groove and found a spot, near a speaker, but not directly in front of it. Near a wall but not closed into a corner. Just right. And we began to dance. At first, it felt awkward, and I was a little self-conscious. I was horribly out of my depth and I had no clue what was going on. But, as we continued to move and I tuned in to the music, it felt good, it felt soooo right, and I went with it. ". . . No man is an island, no man stands alone . . ." sang Dennis Brown. I relaxed in Michaels arm's and once again we began to dance instinctively. It was almost primeval the way we knew how, when and which way each other's body would be moving, before it happened. We just gelled, as my legs turned to jelly. We created a cocoon, that excluded the rest of the world. It was just us. It was alchemy, it was intoxicating, it was . . . over.

On came the lights and quite abruptly, the music was cut. My Mum came in and said that everybody had to leave. Apparently, someone had decided to smoke weed in the toilets and that was a step too far for even her liberal sentiments. We were, after all kids, and she didn't want us breaking the law – yet. Everybody started filing out of the room, moaning and groaning because the party had come to such an abrupt end. I looked at Michael apologetically as my Mum was obviously a little tipsy, and just a bit louder than usual. Her meaty arms were folded, and her face was set. You couldn't reason with her when she was in a mood like that. It was definitely over. "Al yuh cum out!" she said swaying just a little as she ushered people out of the room and down the stairs. I was devastated. I was even more mortified when she shoved a broom into Michaels hands so that he could start cleaning up. I looked at him in alarm and embarrassment and tried to take the broom from him while she wasn't looking. He took it in his stride though and good-naturedly grinned as he grabbed a black bag. Together, we began to tackle the broken plastic cups and empty soft drink tins. I gave the room a cursory glance and stopped. I looked more closely at the wallpaper and saw that there were areas where the flowers had been worn away. "Jesus," I thought. "are you telling me that people rubbed out the wallpaper through dancing?" I was also alarmed to find some empty spirit bottles in the corner behind the speaker, but I kept that to myself and quickly shoved them into the bag. My Mum would have had a fit if she'd have seen the bottles of vodka and brandy in the room. And I made a mental note not to be around when she saw the wallpaper. Luckily, she was making sure that people left quietly so as not to disturb the neighbours.

The fact that we had been blaring out, loud, thumping bass-filled music for hours, and had probably kept the whole street awake, seemed to have escaped her attention. The stifling summer heat hadn't helped, as all the windows had been fully open, for the whole evening. She seemed to have forgotten about that as well. She really was a mass of contradictions when she'd had a drink!

Michael diligently swept up cans and cups in between teasing me and mucking about with Stephanie. I could see my sister and her cronies looking on, shooting me daggers but I didn't care. At one point, my sister tried to get me to tidy the kitchen instead of the living room, which would have kept the way open for her and her mates to access Michael and draw his attention away from me. He quickly offered to help me out in the kitchen as soon as she mentioned it and finally, she got the hint. He wasn't interested in her or her friends, he was actually interested in me. The smile I gave him was so unashamedly delighted that I was sure that I saw a little flush on his cheeks. But boys don't blush I was told, when I mentioned it to him a few days later.

Eventually, when all the hard work of getting the house back to normal had been done, I walked Michael to the front door. Everybody had crashed on the settee or gone to bed while Michael and I sat quietly talking. I looked around after awhile and noticed that we were the only people still awake. As I opened the door, I noticed how late it was. The first birds were starting to sing their morning song and the sky was a gentle blue, with red stripes filtering through as it welcomed the dawn. It was still warm, even though it was early and as I stood on the doorstep,

I knew that I would remember this night for the rest of my life. It became perfect when Michael leaned down towards my lips and gave me my first ever kiss. It was warm, sweet, soft and shit . . . another nosebleed!

"These are my memories. Not to be thought, and lost, and thought again," I said to myself, as I crawled into bed at last. "But to be listened to, and to be learned from. They had come to me on this night, altogether and complete, at the party for a reason. But why?"

And now . . .

Sleep.

***

My wonderful knight in shining armour was, it turned out, just like any other boy in Hackney. After the first flush of love had diminished, I noticed that cracks had started to appear in our 'relationship'. As it was my first encounter with boys, it took a little while for me to spot that my blind adoration wasn't quite reciprocated. He was still able to make me shiver with a look or melt with a kiss, but I don't think I was doing it for him. I was one of life's talkers, someone who had an opinion about everything and wasn't afraid to share them – with the right person. After all, I'd spent a lot of my time with my eyes in a book and my head in the clouds. Not so Michael. He didn't really read and didn't have an opinion on anything other than all things Sea Cadets, which he attended at least three times a week.

At first, I thought it was my crippling shyness that made things awkward, after we kissed, and kissed, and kissed every time we met. I'd close my eyes and melt in his arms and forget about everything except the wonderful feelings that each touch of his lips unlocked. It was magic every time. Beyond that, once I came back down to earth – because I was no longer in his embrace – I was a mess. I struggled to make conversation with him. Maybe it was because I couldn't relax, as we were never alone once I'd opened the front door and ushered him into the house, after our extended snog. My house was always full. My younger siblings kept on giggling and finding reasons to pop into the kitchen where we'd sometimes hang out. My older sister would want to watch telly at exactly the same time that we finally got the living room to ourselves. My Mum was sweet and was happy to have him over, teasing him every time she saw him. She'd look him up and down, and ask, "yuh ever catch cold bwoy, bikaaz your shirt dem buttoned down so low?" Or she'd make a comment about his hair, "bwoy yuh afro look good, yuh mussa spend more time in front da mirror than all my gyals put together." We'd laugh because we knew she was taking the mickey out of him, but seriously, she was so right. He had the most 'enriched' hair that I'd ever come across. It absolutely gleamed with health and product, a perfect halo around his gorgeous face.

One time my Mum said to nobody in particular, "yuh can't trust dem good looking bwoy, yuh know!" None of us responded because even though his name hadn't been called, we all knew she was talking about Michael. We were slouched in the chairs scattered in the living room, all eyes on Lindsay Wagner, the Bionic Woman – my favourite show. We sat there in semi darkness, while the glow of the TV, hypnotic and seductive, whisked us away to another place, another world, another dimension called the future. Not to be outdone by some "half-woman, half-metal creacha" as she called Lindsay, my Mum carried on, as if someone had spoken and she was responding to them. She carried on like she was in the middle of a conversation. " . . . Bikaaz dem man dem can be slippery as hell." I knew a story was coming because she normally broke into patois just before she started. I didn't want to hear it, so what came after that I couldn't say. My eyes and ears were glued to my hero, the bionic woman, who was kicking arse and looking good too. Mum realised that no one was listening and eventually succumbed to watching TV as well.

In retrospect, I wish I'd taken the trouble to listen to my Mum as she usually had a nugget–or–two of sense rolled into her stories. I could tell that things weren't right between me and Michael, and I didn't quite know what to do. I didn't have the nerve to ask my Mum for help. I mean, who did that? She was cool, but not that cool. I considered my options and realised that I didn't have any. I was definitely out of my depth. At the youth club, I'd watch as Michael would come alive with his mates, laughing, joking, and being funny. But not with me. With me, he'd clam up, as did I.

What could I do about it?

I asked my sister for advice. She'd had a heavy, sweaty relationship with a boy two years older than her when she was about fifteen. They spent a lot of time together and seemed to have loads of fun as well as lots in common. They were always smooching, giggling and whispering which was quite annoying to watch and out of character for Sandra. I think she managed to rack up over six months with him which, when you're a kid, is the equivalent of a lifetime. So, one day, I approached the subject of boyfriends with her. I'd been with Michael for a couple of weeks and, well, it wasn't working. I asked her what her secret was, and what I should be doing to keep him interested.

"Just let him do what the hell he likes, and he'll love you forever," were her words of wisdom.

"Erm . . . excuse me? Sorry? How'd you mean?" was my response. I didn't get it. That made no sense. Hell, I knew I was a newbie to the world of love and all that, but somehow, her words of wisdom just didn't feel . . . wise. The word that sprung to mind was that it felt 'slutty'. I instinctively pulled back from the little huddle that we'd created.

When we started the conversation, Sandra could tell from the way that I was hanging on her every word that she had me in the palm of her hands. Then, with her response, she knew that she'd lost me. Big time. We didn't often see eye to eye, and for me to ask for her advice was a big deal. It was one of those rare moments, when we were both on the same page, so I was sure that she wanted to re-establish the bond that we'd had at the start of the conversation. I on the other hand, was desperate, and would've done anything to get her help, to hear what she had to say about all things love and boys. She was doing so well, and I wanted that for myself. But being 'slutty' wasn't the way to go. It was a no no for me.

From the way that I'd pulled out of our 'circle of trust' moment, Sandra knew that she'd messed up, and she tried to back-track and smooth out what she'd said. She covered it with, "whoa, did I say that? Just joking! I didn't mean let them do anything . . ." Her voice trailed off, like she'd fallen off a cliff.

"Well what did you mean?" I asked. I kissed my teeth. "Because it sounded like you were saying that I have to . . . you know," I paused and nodded at her. She looked back blankly.

Eventually she said "No, I don't." She was in the middle of greasing her hair and she held the comb suspended in the air, waiting for me to speak.

"You know . . ." Now it was me falling off the cliff, jumping headfirst, waiting for her to follow my train of thought. She didn't. "Do the . . . tings," I finally said, and she dropped the comb while she looked at me, horrified.

"Do the . . . tings? Are you crazy? What do you think I am?" She thought for a moment, her eyes narrowed to slits and the mood changed. "Are you calling me a whore?" she roared, ready to shake the living daylights out of me. I stepped back instinctively, just in case she decided to follow through.

"No no no, but that's what you said – let him do anything . . ." I nodded and gestured with my hands, encouraging her to finish the sentence. She did, and immediately saw how I'd interpreted it

"For fucks sake! Are you bonkers? I didn't mean that, you plonker" she said, as she gave me a playful shove which sent me half way across the bedroom.

"Okay," I said, "this makes more sense. Just for a minute there it felt like you were saying that I should give up the goods."

"Nah, I didn't mean that – honest!" She laughed again at how we had gotten our wires crossed, and we were friends once more. She went back to doing her hair, parting it and adding Afro Sheen along the groove, carefully working the moisture up the shaft. She started talking about her latest crush and I realised that I'd just have to be patient, as I really needed her to tell me the real secrets of her success. I was pretty much out of ideas when it came to Michael, so I carried on smiling even though I was starting to feel that she might not have been as all-knowing as I'd thought. Unfortunately, after hanging around for half an hour, I realised that nothing else was coming my way. Her words of wisdom were, well . . . her words of wisdom. "Let him do what the hell he likes – apart from sex – and he'll love you forever," was as good as it got!

As I got ready for bed later that evening, I thought about what Sandra said, and had to admit that she did have a string of guys after her. Okay, so her relationships seemed to be really short-lived, but, she must have been doing something right I reasoned. I picked up the Sidney Sheldon book by the side of my bed and began to read. Eventually, I let it flop down and rest on my chest as I realised that I'd re-read the same page four times. My thoughts turned back to Sandra, and I wondered if there was a grain of truth in her attitude towards relationships. She never seemed to be stressed out like some of the girls in her click were, always crying and bleating on about their 'man dem' letting them down. I chewed it over some more and decided that she seemed to know what she was talking about. As I didn't have anything else to go on, it made sense to follow her instructions to the letter.

Over the following weeks, I didn't bat an eyelid when Michael did or said things that were a little off, a little questionable. Like when he went to cadets four times in one week because he had a marching parade and played football on Thursday and Sunday then went to watch Arsenal play on Saturday. This meant that I only saw him three times in two weeks for a couple of hours. And, on our last date, we'd planned to meet at the local youth club called Toc H, and he turned up an hour late. I was crazy mad that he didn't seem to want to hook up any longer and was so casual about being late. I'd spent an age getting ready – wearing my pink crew neck from Marks and Sparks and my brown polka-dot pleated skirt from my Mum's Littlewoods catalogue – and was not comfortable with being treated like what seemed like an afterthought.

I'd had enough, and when I checked in with my sister, after the Toc H incident, she wasn't exactly one hundred percent behind me. "Yeah," she admitted, "I get it that you're a bit pissed off, and, you know what? It does make me feel crappy that they treat me like that sometimes. But all the boys are like that, so I don't take it personally anymore."

"Er, okay then, I'll stick with it,' I muttered quietly, while my mind was screaming, "Are you crazy? Can we show a little self-respect here Sandra?" Apparently . . . not, was what I came up with. But, I still held out because I thought Michael was special, that he was different, so I just couldn't leave it like that. Surely this isn't how it's supposed to be. I thought that when you met someone, you'd talk to each other, enjoy each other, and have fun together. I wasn't ready to give up on my ideal, my image of what a great relationship should look like, so I asked, "What about that guy you were with for ages? You know . . . the one that you were lovey dovey with, and couldn't stop kissing?" I knew I was whining, but I couldn't help myself. I wanted to believe . . . that love existed, and that being with a guy added something good to my life.

"You mean Leroy?" she asked with a scoff. "He was weird. All he wanted to do was talk. Hold hands and talk some more. He drove me bonkers, but he was such a good kisser." She paused and straightened her tights as they were sticking up her bum. I waited for her and we continued walking across the Common to Victoria Park. A fair had set up, and we were going to check it out. Then she added, "he wasn't normal that's for sure, and the only reason he lasted that long was because he used to spend a fortune on me." I was gutted.

"Maybe I had it all wrong," I said to myself as I listened to her words. It made me think about all the shitty relationships that my Mum had had over the years and I sighed. I gave in. This was obviously how relationships work. So, I didn't protest, I didn't object, I didn't call Michael out on anything or challenge him in any way. And, after a few more tortured weeks . . . I didn't have a boyfriend any longer. I was dumped. I didn't see it coming and was heart-broken. When Sandra found me hiding out in my room, sobbing, wet and sad, she knew the score instantly and comforted me with, "arrh . . . did he dump you?"

"Yes," I said, and poured out my heart to her while she listened uncomfortably for twenty minutes.

"Well, at least he did it himself and didn't send his friend to do it for him," she said, in a sort of caring tone. I stopped crying, blinked, and looked at her with daggers in my eyes.

"How could you think that's a good thing to say Sandra? I resumed my tears, wailing and crying even harder.

"Whaaattt . . ." she said, eyes wide and innocent, ". . . happened to me loads of times." She tried a different approach. "Girl you got off lightly. I was talking to Sarah McDonald the other day," she paused, and I carried on crying. She continued regardless. "You know, the one with gap teeth?" I eventually looked at her blankly. "Anyway, she'd been going out with Johnny for three months and when he dumped her, he didn't even bother to tell her! She just saw him at a party in Tottenham, filling his mouth with Daisy Price. When she called him out on it, he pretended that he didn't know her. Looked at her like she was some crazy psycho bitch with a case of mistaken identity – I kid you not! Three months they had. Huh." Sandra stopped talking, hands on hips, as she realised that I'd stopped listening, and was crying again. Louder. I really didn't care about Sarah's – whatever her name was – pain at that moment. Sandra finally saw that there was no helping me. So, she left me to cry and die in peace.

A few weeks later, while talking to Stephanie, I found that I still couldn't mention Michael's name without bursting into tears. I couldn't understand why I had no control over myself and was acting like a lovesick teenager from a Mills and Boons romantic novel. I told her my predicament. We sat in the lush grass, leaning against an ancient tree in the Common located at the end of my road. It was a surprisingly warm summer's day, and I could see the quiet swish and sway of leaves blowing gently in the soft warm breeze. Across the way from us, pigeons were pecking around looking for crumbs of food, while a few kids were playing about, kicking ball and squealing like little pigs in a blanket. In the background I heard an ice cream van, his tinny music announcing that he was in the neighbourhood. I thought about getting an ice lolly but decided against it, as I couldn't be bothered. I didn't have the energy for anything anymore.

I'd dragged Stephanie to my favourite park so that I could find a private place to be miserable. We sat in silence for awhile and then I blurted out that I thought I was losing it, as Michael was basically all I thought about. I was a mess in the way that I'd only seen on telly. I could see it in my mind, unfolding . . .

. . . *Story – just in, here on BBC News.*

A fifteen-year-old black girl was found in the east end
of London, dead from a broken heart. When asked about
the incident, her family all agreed that she was a sensitive
soul who couldn't get over her break up with her boyfriend,
Michael. Her mother said it was really sad and
that she'd be missed . . .

My 'Problem Page' entry in Jackie would look like this:

Dear Jackie,
My boyfriend has dumped me, and I don't know
what to do? Help!!!
Lovesick from Hackney

I was behaving like it was the end of the world, and I couldn't understand why. What was wrong with me? Real people – living outside of the world of telly and teen magazines – didn't act like this. I'd never seen Sandra fall apart over the break-up of her relationships. Sure, she was down for a day or two, but then, she moved on to the next. It was clear from the advice that she dished out that she pretty much had no clue when it came to love, and I realised that she didn't really take it seriously, or take it to heart, like I did. In fact, the more I thought about it, I became aware that I'd never seen my Mum getting cut up over her 'boyfriends'. She didn't cry or mope about at all. Okay, so she drank a little more than usual for a while, but not for long as she never had a problem finding another fella. "Good riddance, onwards and upwards," is what she'd say after a breakup. So why couldn't I be more like them, I wondered? Even Granny kept it together, with her older and dignified 'gentleman friends'. They were around for awhile – in the background, never introduced or included, nothing major or permanent – and then they weren't. No emotion shown when she was with or without them, or when they broke up.

I had to admit that the women in my family were my role models, as they were bad-arse black women that I admired. So, what the hell was wrong with me! I was secretly disgusted with myself because I couldn't keep it together and get over Michael in a less dramatic way. I'd seen myself as having front as well, as being hardcore, and was unprepared for the emotional avalanche that came from mingling with one boy. No matter how I tried to twist it, I could only be described as a wimp.

Stephanie was a real help in my time of trouble because she didn't judge or offer useless advice. She also had the inside scoop on all things Michael because she was his cousin, which was a real bonus. As we sat together in the Common, I realised that she had become a real saviour. I swatted a fly, and we watched the kids throw a frisbee up into the air. They started squealing and shouting as it had become stuck in a tree. "Michael said that he found you attractive because you weren't like most girls," Stephanie said, as I once again turned our conversation to my broken heart.

"Really?" I said with surprise, as I didn't see myself as so different. I looked at the tree and the kids milling around and thought about helping to get the frisbee down. Then I changed my mind as I couldn't be bothered to get up.

"Yep," said Stephanie. "He thought that because you read a lot and you didn't go on about what most girls talked about . . . you know, clothes and makeup and that kind of stuff, that you were different. He couldn't understand why you changed." I thought about it for a while and found that he was right. I had changed. I'd stopped being a 'person' and started being a 'girlfriend'. I didn't have a clue what being a girlfriend meant, and I'd become more and more tongue tied and self-conscious. I looked back over the last couple of weeks and realised that by taking my sister's advice, I'd effectively lost ninety percent of my personality. Stephanie finished off with, "I thought you should know as I'm sorry that it didn't work out with you guys." That information stuck with me and struck a deep chord. I mulled it around for awhile and realised that although his words were harsh, Michael was right. I'd stopped being me. And, as a result, I could see that he did what any self-respecting boy would do – he dumped me. Ouch!

What happened next? Well, I began to heal. It took a little while, but I was finally able to think about other things – and not just Michael. I was no longer blinded by Cupid's arrow, and I began to see a few of the rough edges that Michael had, which had been invisible to me before. I watched from a distance, at our usual Monday Club, as he flirted and circled around certain girls, drawing them into his area of influence, before pouncing on them. And then, I watched as they became a couple, inseparable for awhile, flaunting their love – or so it seemed to me. Everywhere that I looked, there he was, smiling that beautiful smile and I would ache, and watch from a distance, miserable, hurt and disillusioned because he was having a good time, and I was not. I couldn't breathe, and then one day, I found that I could. I found that I could watch him from a distance and no longer feel anything much. Don't get me wrong, I was still sore, but I was able to focus on other things, other people, after awhile.

Stephanie and I became good friends. I even began to think that the most important relationship that I had during my time with Michael, was in fact with his cousin. Michael turned out to be just a diversion. Once I got over the kisses, I realised that being with him wasn't a whole lot of fun, and that being in a relationship wasn't what I thought it would be. Clearly, I didn't know much about real life couples, but even I knew that it wasn't supposed to play itself out in us being tongue tied and tortured. But, he was, my very first love, which had been all-consuming and emotional – even if it only lasted for a little while.

I continued to observe Michael from a distance at first with jealousy, and then with distain. I realised that he was a bit of a ladies man, who had many different girlfriends on the go, all at once, all the time. Stephanie was a bit pissed at him, as she had initially thought that he was a 'keeper', a great guy to have as a boyfriend. She quickly realised that there was more to him than he let on, and one night, she confessed that she thought he was, "a man whore, who liked the chase." I couldn't really argue with that, and I was relieved that I wasn't on his radar anymore. It was hard to swallow that I was just another girl that he happened to like for two minutes before he lost interest and moved on to the next. But, I didn't say anything negative about him, as he was Stephanie's cousin after all. We never talked about Michael after that and concentrated instead on our friendship. As for boys? Well, I sure as hell didn't take my sister's advice on relationships ever again and I also decided to leave love alone and focus on other things, until I was a little older.

Sixteen

S ixteen was an important year for me as many aspects of my life which had previously plagued me, changed. Surprisingly, my nosebleeds, fevers, and cold sores, diminished over time. My doctor, who replaced Dr Patel, was very proactive in trying to understand my illness. Medication helped with my fevers, and eventually a wonderful, transparent ointment came to the rescue which was brilliant at zapping those clusters of cold sores, before they had a chance to ruin my face. They still looked ugly when they did come up, but at least my lips weren't purple and crusty anymore.

As for my nosebleeds? After a series of cauterises, which didn't help, and lots of back and forth to hospital, Hereditary Haemorrhagic Telangiectasia (HHT) explained my difficulties with blood loss, throughout my childhood. Knowing this didn't change anything for me on the surface, but it was as if a lightbulb had been switched on in my brain and things made sense.

I remembered when my Granny once said, "Tante Flo was a bleeder like you, lord that girl could fill a river with blood." I didn't give it much thought at the time because, let's face it, Tante Flo was a great aunt who lived a million miles away in Trinidad, who I'd never met, and wasn't ever likely to meet. Plus, Granny also said it in passing, as if it was no big deal, like walking around with a trolley in a supermarket or, deciding to do the washing up after dinner. That annoyed me. It wasn't a good time as I was tetchy, and a little upset about once again missing Bionic Woman. I remember thinking, "Do I care that your sister could fill a river with blood? No, not really – it isn't a competition for christ sake!" But I never said that. Those were private thoughts that I kept to myself as I knew what I could or wouldn't say when talking with Granny. Speaking well was important to her and with one look she would wither you to the ground, if you spoke or acted out of turn. She would make you feel like you were such a disappointment, that a slapping would be preferable to that look.

So, HHT was a revelation to me, but changed nothing in the way that my family treated me. I wasn't even sure that my Mum really registered the information when I told her. As I was old enough to go to the hospital appointments by myself, she'd stopped asking how things were going in that department, as it never changed, whatever they did. It was like it was one less chore for her to deal with, and she left it up to me to manage it.

I'd been looking after my health on my own since I was a kid, and I'd hoped that having HHT would prove to my family that I really had an illness. That it wasn't 'just me having 'another nosebleed'. But nope. It wasn't on anybody's radar anymore, except mine. Because my news had had such a lukewarm response with my family, I didn't share it with anyone else. When I told Sandra, she looked at me blankly – and that was it. Not in that horrible stare that she'd give me when she caught me wearing her clothes without asking. No. It was more of a 'okay, thanks for sharing, but I've nothing to add to this conversation', kind of look. Everybody else, responded in a similar way. So, I let it go. Nosebleeds had been a constant preoccupation in my world all my life, but it wasn't important to anybody else. That realisation was hurtful and once again made me feel isolated and forgotten. But, not for long. As I thought about where I was with my illness, I realised that things had changed. The physical side had altered loads as the bleeding had started to recede after the 'party incident' when I was fifteenth. And even though it hadn't stopped completely, things had definitely quietened down.

Over the years, I'd come to believe that I'd caused my nosebleeds. Anger, resentment, and fear were all emotions that I felt before, during, and after these occurrences. And, I thought that my negativity and lack of control over these emotions was the cause of each nosebleed. It was just too hard to untangle how I was feeling from the actual event. As I got older, I let puberty and maturity guide my body, my feelings and my nosebleeds – and things changed. I started to relax and feel free. The gap between incidents gave me hope, and as I started to chill and feel like I was normal – BAM! I would have a nosebleed for half an hour. It pissed me off, but I slowly got a handle on things.

Knowing that I had an illness, allowed me to disentangle my emotions from what was happening to me physically. It was messed up. Because, when I'd become angry and bleed, I'd assumed over time that my anger had caused the bleeding. I was starting to realise that while my emotions happened at the same time, they weren't really linked, other than through timing. So, it wasn't my fault that nosebleeds happened. They just – happened!

It sounds so simple but, as I began to learn about why my life was filled with illness, I started to see cracks, and understand how complex it was. I even wondered why my emotional state was never really taken seriously by my family, my doctors, my teachers – by anybody. The confusion of feeling caused me so much torment over the years and, I wish I'd found my childhood voice earlier and had been able to express the way that I'd felt. I'd truly believed that I was damaged goods. Until I met Stephanie, properly, at my sister's birthday party. Before her, I hadn't heard of anyone else who had nosebleeds and she helped me feel less like a freak and a little more ordinary. I'd had to work hard to find this new sense of normal, as, I'd spent a lifetime feeling something else. It was a sinking feeling, a sense of drowning that I didn't quite know what to do with.

I could always swim, but not far, as while I'd had lessons at school from an early age, it wasn't consistent, and I never practised. Swimming was not really a thing that black people did. "Eena dat dutty sea and dat nasty pool full of bleach? Now why would I put fi mi self eena dat confusion? No suh, nutten good can come from dat," was how one of my Mum's friends put it. And, more to the point, it cost money which we didn't have. But, once in a while, during the summer holidays, I'd go to the Lido with Sandra. We went to either Victoria Park, London Fields, or Highbury Corner. It had to be a boiling hot day, and, not a lot of swimming took place. There was dunking and bombing and playing tag, with loads of splashing as too many bodies crammed themselves into the open-air pool. Over time I became confident in swimming short distances, but I could never float. Never. I sunk like a stone.

Lesson after lesson at school and with friends showed me that while I could tread water for a second, I'd slowly descend to the bottom of the pool, which at the deep end, scared the shit out of me. So, I'd mask it, by hanging on to the side of the pool as much as possible. Or, by swimming for dear life to make sure that I never ended up stuck in the middle, without something, or someone, to hang onto. My sinking was as inevitable as my hair shrinkage as soon as it touched water. Both just happened, and I learnt to accept it. Nobody could find a reason for my sinking. It was just accepted. And after a while they skated over teaching me and made sure that I stayed in the shallows. No doubt carrying all my psychological baggage around, didn't help to lighten my load. Jeez, what a mess I was!

I'm not sure how, but over the years I've managed to navigate my way through everything that was thrown at me. Some of it was shed as part of the rough and tumble of growing up, while other parts remain buried, deep, so as not to interfere with my daily life. But every now and then, those deep feelings that I carried around for all my years of being me, pop out. And I either explode, explore it, make sense of it, or I shove it back into hiding – without having a nosebleed. As I sometimes look back on my past, I'm proud of how I handled myself. Way too much of a burden for a child to carry around.

***

Everyone's moved on, everything's moved on. Hell, even I've moved on as I'm now sixteen and about to start college. And, I've realised that I'm not burdened by an illness which consumed me when I was a child. New beginnings.

I've worked hard at being less nerdy and discovered other interests such as music and art which worked wonders on my self-esteem and my sense of self. I feel calm and at peace mostly and I don't get into such a tizzy when I can't speak out properly, or cope in new situations. I take a deep breath, get all flustered on the inside, get through it on the outside, and slowly calm down altogether. I'm also more tolerant, and don't get as frustrated or angry with myself or with other people anymore. Outwardly, there isn't a lot of difference between the fifteen-year-old and sixteen-year-old version of me because I'm not the kind of person to draw unnecessary attention to myself, if I can help it. And to be honest, my highs and lows can all look the same to people who don't know and understand me. But, I've definitely changed for the better – no doubt about it!

Throughout it all though, I've had help. My secret weapon has always there, keeping me safe and making things work regardless. I am blessed with a support network that can help me iron out my kinks and point me, sort of, in the right direction. I have a Granny that has taken a genuine interest in all her grandchildren, who had the intelligence and patience to support each of us, in whatever way was needed. For me, she's provided a safety valve through talking. From my early years, I expressed myself through chatter and she let me prattle on. As I grew older, our dialogue became a way of letting off steam and shooting the breeze about anything and everything. I hadn't realised just how much I relied on her support until I started making my own friends when I was fifteen. Before that, she and my Mum were tag team wrestlers – Giant Haystacks and Big Daddy – with my Mum providing the practical day-to-day support and Granny filling in the gaps and cracks. With Sandra, Granny would tell stories and instil our family history from Trinidad and America where her brother and some of her sisters had settled. For the younger ones, she was Father Christmas and baby-sitter all rolled into one – bringing gifts in her bottomless goody bag. She also brought money, food or both and was a lifeline that my Mum regularly pulled on. In between my Mum and Granny, were my Mum's friends. They were strong independent black women who pooled their lives, and resources to make things work on a shoestring budget for their children, and for us. I can't imagine how colourless my life would have been without them. In fact, I can't imagine how colourless I would have been without them.

Over time, my confidence has grown and so has my friendship group. I've started dance lessons and, as Sandra and I are no longer joined at the hip because of my Mum, I've branched out and started doing lots of other things without her. I've crept out of my shell and found that I can't fit back into it! So, I've stayed out in the open and feel less afraid and more comfortable with people, in all situations. I've become more talkative, and an even better listener, and instead of hiding in the background, I've found my voice and I'm not afraid to use it, sometimes. I suppose in essence, I've become a decluttered, ordinary, adolescent. I've come through, and out the other side of my journey of childhood, self-discovery, and illness. Life is good.

Until another set of curveballs are thrown in my direction. But that's another story . . .